Nudists Die Too

Louise Lang

PublishAmerica
Baltimore

First printing

ISBN: 1-4137-2427-2
PUBLISHED BY PUBLISHAMERICA, LLLP
www.publishamerica.com
Baltimore

Printed in the United States of America

To my special companion/love, and to all the relatives and friends who cheered me on in the creation of this novel, particularly those dedicated writers whose thoughtful critiques helped me along.

NOTES AND ACKNOWLEDGMENTS

Adam's Peak is a work of fiction, and its characters are, with the exception of public figures mentioned in passing, my own creations. With regard to its geographical settings, the novel makes use of both real and fictional places and takes certain liberties with the former. The violent incident that occurs in Chapter 11 is loosely based on the 1996 bombing of Colombo's Central Bank; however, the date and specific details of that event have been altered. The quotation in the novel's opening section comes from James Emerson Tennent's *Ceylon: an Account of the Island / Physical, Historical, and Topographical / with Notices of its Natural History, Antiquities and Productions* (London: Longman, 1859).

I am indebted to the many people who shared their knowledge, expertise, and time with me as I wrote this book. In particular I would like to thank Malinda Abeykoon, Ann Burt, David Burt, Andrew Buultjens, Monica Büültjens, Afton Cayford, Katherine Headrick, Sally Headrick, Amitha Kothalawala, John Morris, Zoe Pagnamenta, Asela Pilapitiya, Sharon Salloum, Mervyn Shedden, Primrose Shedden, and Rikardo Shedden. All of these kind people have assisted me enormously; any errors, however, are my own.

I'm very grateful for the enthusiasm and intelligent guidance of Hilary McMahon and Alison Hardacre at Westwood Creative Artists and Barry Jowett and Andrea Waters of Dundurn. Many thanks as well to my parents, Andrew and Glenna Burt, for their long-standing support and encouragement. Finally, I am especially grateful to Paul Headrick, whose contributions to this project are immeasurable.

Speaking of Sri Lanka, these peace talks with the Norwegians sound promising. The ceasefire seems to be holding in any case, and the government and the LTTE look to be on reasonably civil terms with each other (though my aunt is still skeptical). You probably get much better coverage of this stuff in the UK than I'm getting over here. Or am I just being apathetic and lazy??

Anyway, speaking of laziness, I should get to the pile of marking I've been avoiding for the past week. Argh. It's the home stretch, though. Hey, did I tell you I joined a cricket league? An out-of-shape and overweight lot we are, but it's a blast. Good luck with the big recital! Let me know how it goes.
As ever,
Rudy

P.S. Adam says don't worry about the jacket. He'd forgotten all about it. But if I happened to be passing through your neighbourhood this summer, could I pick it up?

NUDISTS DIE TOO

LOUISE LANG

CHAPTER 1

Sparrows were twittering and chirping as daylight cut brilliant wedges into the bedroom's darkness where the heavy drapes didn't quite meet one another. The figure in the bed was restless and sweaty, having slept but little, all night turning and shifting, thoughts running round and round like a hamster on a wheel. *I'll have to kill her. That's all there is to it. I'll have to kill her. God knows I'm not a killer, but I can't see any other way.*

"Help! Call 9-1-1!" Doreen Pierce ran shouting — down the hill, away from the gathering crowd, her pendulous tanned breasts swinging, belly flab jiggling, and brown eyes wide.

Hot, dry weather pressed down on the elderly olive grove that sprawled over the acreage known as Olive Canyon Nudist Resort in Southern California.

"Dom, call 9-1-1! A man collapsed at the tennis court." Seeing her husband's signal that he understood, she turned and rushed back up the dirt road.

Dominic Pierce called the emergency number. Then he paged the gatekeeper.

White-haired Howard Brill entered the room. Dominic said, "Howard, I'm going to the tennis courts. A man collapsed. Hold down the fort while I'm gone. Shouldn't be long," and rushed out, jumping his mountain bike into motion.

Howard watched Dom, thinking the man, the club's

7

manager, was okay for his age. At fifty, he was over six feet tall with a wiry build and only a slightly-receding hairline. Howard craned his neck to see what was happening up the hill, but the tennis courts were about a quarter mile up the serpentine dirt road.

A glance at the fallen man told Doreen it was too late. His wife sat on the lawn next to him, sobbing and stroking his face.

A man approached Doreen saying, "I'm a doctor. I saw what happened. There was nothing that could be done for him—he was gone before he hit the ground. I checked him."

"Thanks," she said, pushing her pink-framed sunglasses up on the bridge of her nose. She glanced at her friend Ruby, the copper-skinned beauty weeping next to the deceased. Doreen pushed a wisp of dark hair from her face with fingers ending in stubby fingernails. "Excuse me, but I think Ruby needs me," she said as she turned away.

Doreen knelt next to the new widow. "Ruby, I'm so sorry about Elliott. The paramedics are on their way. Is there anything I can do to help?" She put her arm around the distraught woman's naked shoulders, feeling the coolness of the lush lawn on her bare skin and the welcome shade from the many olive trees.

Doreen's question pulled Ruby from her private agony. She looked up with tortured eyes, her lovely face contorted, and finger-combed a long strand of silver-streaked red hair.

"What will I tell them back in Indiana? About where he died, I mean. I can't tell them he died after playing tennis with nothing on but his sneakers! They don't know we're nudists." Ruby wiped at tears with the back of her hand.

"I'm sure your family won't give it a second thought if you tell them you were camping at Olive Canyon Resort. They won't know it's a nudist resort. No need to mention what he was, or wasn't, wearing," Doreen said gently, moving her arm off Ruby's shoulder to hold one of her friend's hands.

"Yes. You're right of course. They won't know. I guess I need to make some calls. Can I use the phone in the office?" Middle-aged, Ruby was slim, with a figure that defied gravity.

Dom Pierce arrived, propped his bike on its kickstand. "Sure. Come on."

Ruby started to follow him to the office. She glanced back a few times at Elliott's motionless form on the ground as if that might make him start breathing again.

"No. Wait! I can't leave him yet. I can make the calls later," she said, running back to the inert figure, and settling down beside him again. She stroked his pallid face, unable to believe what had happened, seeming to watch from somewhere else—it was all so unreal. She knew she must go through the motions, do what had to be done. But she knew she'd awaken soon from this nightmare, and Elliott would be alive.

Fifteen or twenty people wearing only hats, shoes, and sunglasses, stood quietly watching, murmuring condolences. Tennis courts, unnaturally empty, lacked their usual *thwack, thwack* sounds. Even the normally boisterous children were silent, curious. It was as if the hushed scene waited in the heat for the director's cue for action.

A freckly boy of about seven with a gap in his front teeth shoved his way through the forest of legs. "Is he really dead?" His innocent question startled Ruby.

"Yes, he's really dead." Tears burned.

"My grampa died once." He plopped himself next to Ruby, looking sad. Ruby put an arm around his sun-warmed little back and pulled him closer. He looked up at her eyes and said, "I miss him."

Dominic reached the gate just in time to tell the paramedic unit where to find the victim. The boxy vehicle roared away toward the tennis courts, lights flashing and sirens blaring, leaving clouds of gray-brown dust hanging in the breathless air.

The paramedics, Jack and Arnie, both in their early twenties, arrived where Elliott Falstaff lay. Someone had covered him with a sheet. Arnie, built like a piano-mover with a long, brown tied-back mane, hauled out the gurney, setting it on the lawn. He and Jack, a super hunk, carefully placed the body on the stretcher, and loaded it into the vehicle. As they went about their business, both men seared into memory what was, to them, an extraordinary scene, glancing surreptitiously at the unclad club members.

Soon the crowd dispersed except for a few people. The paramedics drove slowly—not in any hurry to leave—back to the gate where they had entered.

Traveling the highway Arnie said, "I think I'll go back there some day soon. You ever been there before?" He nudged his partner in the ribs, grinning slyly.

"No, but I'm goin' back too. Count on it." Jack slapped his thigh for emphasis.

"Let's go together on our next day off."

"We can't," Jack said, shaking his blond head. "There was a sign. Couples (married or single) only beyond this gate—NO exceptions."

"Maybe we can talk some girls into going with us. How 'bout Amy? She's pretty adventurous."

"Yeah, that might work. Perhaps Nita would go for it, too."

CHAPTER 2

Just two days before he had a heart attack and died at Olive Canyon, Elliott Falstaff had spent a day with a few of his commercial-airline pilot cronies. This annual event was planned well ahead and anticipated eagerly. While the men were thus occupied, his wife Ruby, with friends Veronica Corrigan and Doreen Pierce, took *Windcatcher* out for a sail. *Windcatcher* was the Pierce's twenty-seven-foot white fiberglass sloop.

The previous day Doreen had called her cousin Veronica. "Tomorrow Ruby and I are getting together. We're hoping you can spend some time with us, Ronnie." Doreen was nibbling on a chocolate bar. "We'll do something fun, like take the boat out for a sail. You wanna come with us?"

"Sure. Love to. Sounds great. What'll we do if there's no wind?" For Veronica, always a contingency plan.

"We can use the engine. I've been kinda down since Dom's been away. It'll be good to get away from everything, don't you think?"

"Absolutely. Call me in the morning when you're ready."

Blue sky and a nice breeze—perfect for a sail, and Doreen was ready. Home seemed different and lonely without Dominic's presence, but peaceful and somehow more pleasant. A couple of evenings ago, Dom had had one Manhattan too many, lost his temper, and stomped out to go to Olive Canyon for a while, after telling Doreen he'd return in a day or two.

Ruby and Veronica drove into the Long Beach Marina's parking lot right behind Doreen. Together they carried lunches and gear down the long boardwalk to the boat. They loaded everything onto the side deck and climbed aboard, transferring the pile down into the cockpit.

With the hatch unlocked and opened, they went below to get sails. The cabin had a tiny sink, cabinets, and stove in the galley, a small table with benches, a minuscule head, and a fair-sized V berth occupying the forward area up to the sail locker. Compact and efficient, nevertheless, four people could sleep in the cabin by converting the table area into a double bed. Two non-opening portholes on each side admitted light and provided view.

"Have you sailed much on little sloops like this?" Doreen asked Ruby. Doreen and Veronica had sailed together many times, with and without their husbands.

"Some. Elliott and I rent boats to sail over to Catalina."

"Good. Then you probably know port from starboard, the main from the jib, sheets and halyards, and all that good stuff."

Ruby nodded. Doreen hauled the jib out of its sail bag, handing it to her friend. She grabbed three life vests from the storage area and headed up the companionway, with Veronica and Ruby following. Veronica had a slightly noticeable limp. Her right lower leg had been replaced by a prosthesis.

On deck they got the jib ready, leaving it down until the time was right. As a team they removed the blue canvas mainsail cover and stowed it below.

"Okay, we're about ready," Doreen said. "When I get the engine started, Ronnie, you take the helm while Ruby and I unfasten the lines from the dock cleats." Looking at Ruby she said, "Undo the bow line, and heave it on board. Hold onto the boat's rail, and hop aboard. Got that? I'll take care of the stern line."

"Aye, aye, skipper!" Ruby saluted, laughing, jumping down to the dock. "I haven't had this much fun in ages and ages. Let her rip, Cap'n. Let's cast off. Don't you just love all this nautical talk?"

Ruby giggled, saluted, and grabbed the bow line. Doreen tended the stern line.

Veronica grinned and nodded. The gas engine grumbled to life at a turn of the key. Ruby did exactly as ordered. With the lines and the women back aboard, and one hand guiding the tiller, Veronica shifted into reverse. Ruby and Doreen sat with her. She set the throttle very low, and *Windcatcher* responded by backing gently out of the slip. A slight turn, a shift into forward gear, and the boat started down the long canal leading to Long Beach Harbor.

Doreen's exuberant "Yahoo!" was accompanied by the soft churning of the water aft and the persistent drone of the small inboard engine.

"Yahoo!" echoed Ruby. "We're off. Row, row, row your boat, gently down the stream," she sang out. The other two joined her in a couple of choruses.

After the narrow channel widened into the harbor, Doreen said, "The wind feels like it's enough to set the sails." Looking at Veronica she said, "Ronnie, you steer while we hoist the sails. Okay?"

"Great. This is really fun."

Ruby followed Doreen forward. On the fore deck they first loosened the main sheet a bit, then raised the main. As soon as the sail filled, the sloop heeled over to port and picked up speed. Ruby left Doreen on the bow pulling up the jib. Stepping down into the cockpit, she shut off the engine. Hearing only the quiet tickling of water along the hull—moving ahead without the engine, a joyous moment for rag sailors—the women sighed with pleasure. The salty smell was invigorating.

On the foredeck, Doreen set the jib to catch the breezes. The knot meter told them their speed was five knots, very satisfactory in the light breeze.

"We did it. Yay, team!" Ruby was clearly having fun, as were the cousins. Ruby had taken over at the tiller.

"Would you like me to take the tiller for a while?" Doreen asked, settling onto the padded bench at the cockpit's stern.

"No. This is fun. I'll let you know when I need a break. Did you both remember to use sunscreen this morning?"

"Sure. It's a habit. Did you?" Doreen adjusted her sunglasses, then dug a chocolate bar out of her bag of stuff. Peeling off the wrapper at one end, she held it out to her companions.

Taking some chocolate, Ruby said, "Yeah, I always wear sunscreen. What'd you bring for lunch? I have PB & J sandwiches, and fruit. If you want any, help yourself." Ruby's sailing experience was obvious—she kept the boat at just the right angle to the wind so the sails stayed filled. Her coppery skin glistened, her face glowed.

"Thanks. I have PB & honey, same difference, I guess. Fruit, and plenty of these babies." Doreen waved her small remnant of candy.

"I brought pretty much the same stuff," Veronica said, then told them one of her jokes. She looked so cute with her big hat tied under her chin, and a grin on her pretty face, that Doreen fished in her stuff bag and pulled out her camera. They took turns taking snapshots of each other in pairs.

Ruby said, "Tell me, where do you think Dom went?"

"I'm sure he's at the mobile home at Olive Canyon. He'll be sober in the morning and will see things differently. This isn't the first time he's done this."

"He left you before?" Ruby didn't know the Pierces as well as Veronica did, and seemed shocked by Dominic's behavior.

"Yes. But he comes back. He gets nasty when he's full of booze."

"That's too bad. Does he ever hit you?"

"No. I don't think he ever would." To change the subject Doreen said, "Look. Look at that buoy—it's loaded with harbor seals. Aren't they cute!" She thought, *Dom has his problems, especially with alcohol. I've never considered leaving him, even though he thinks nothing of leaving me for a few days now and then. He doesn't care how I feel about it. Maybe I should give some thought to leaving him for a while, or even permanently. Maybe we'd both be better off.*

"They sure are cute," said Veronica. "I've wasted a pile of film on them in recent years."

After they had sailed past the breakwater and were outside the protected harbor, the freighter traffic was much less threatening. Now able to be less vigilant, they opened their insulated coolers to enjoy a meal together, taking turns steering.

"So, Dory, how's your business going?" asked Veronica between bites of sandwich.

"It's terrific, now that I have a good staff." Looking at Veronica she said, "Did I tell you we're putting on a Large Women's Fashion Show in a couple of weeks?" Doreen took a sip of ice water. Her gaze went to Ruby. "My right-hand person is a man, a gay, who does so much for me, and takes care of a lot of details. I'd be lost without him."

"No, you hadn't told me. Will we be able to attend?" Veronica asked, indicating Ruby as the other part of the "we" with a slight incline of her head.

"Sure, if you really want to." Her chocolate bar bit the dust. "I didn't mention it in previous years—I didn't think you'd enjoy this sort of show. Big women, I mean."

Ruby asked, "Is your business limited to large women's fashions?"

"Yup. That's why I'm not sure you'd like my show. You two together don't weigh as much as one of our models." She laughed.

"I'd love to see your creations, Doreen, even if they're not my size. As a designer, you're probably very talented." Ruby took a bite of her peach. "You know, I've never seen your work, and I'd like to."

"Okay. I'll be expecting to see you at the show."

They had sailed about halfway to Catalina Island when they agreed it was time to turn around and head back. They tacked neatly and came about. Soon they sighted the outer harbor breakwater.

"Doreen! Look!"

A massive black freighter loomed above them on a collision course.

"They don't see us!" Veronica was standing now, flapping a towel, hoping to make them more visible to the ship.

Doreen twisted the ignition key, crammed the lever forward, shoved the throttle to max. She steered hard to starboard. The sails slatted uselessly. The behemoth crashed through the water to port, unaware of the drama below. Saltwater sprayed the cockpit and its occupants.

"You did it, Doreen! You pulled us out."

"Wow! Too close, much too close." Doreen's look of intense concentration did not relax until the freighter was some distance away. Then she shut down the engine, to sail again with the light wind. She pulled out a chocolate bar.

"What's that white thing floating in the water behind us?" Veronica asked, going to the stern and hanging over to get a good look. "It looks like a very long train to a wedding gown. It's a great big sheet of plastic! Musta got caught in the prop when you ran the engine just now."

Doreen abandoned the tiller to see for herself. "That thing must be twenty feet long and twelve or fifteen feet wide. We'll have to get rid of it somehow, or we won't be able to run the engine." Doreen went to the controls saying, "I'll turn it on and put it in reverse. Maybe that'll unwind the plastic off the prop." She did so. "Is it off yet?"

"No. Still there."

"I'll hafta go down and pull it off." Doreen went down to the cabin and fetched her underwater goggles and a sharp paring knife. She changed from shorts and T-shirt to a swimsuit. On deck again she said, "Now is the time I wish I had some scuba gear and knew how to use it.

Watch for sharks. If you spot any, bang hard on the hull so I can hear it."

She climbed over the transom and lowered her legs into the ocean. "That's cold!" She sucked in as much air as she could, and pushed herself down along the outside of the stern. She hacked at the offending material as close to the propeller as possible, but very soon surfaced for air. Veronica and Ruby, diligent in their shark-watch, were anxious to see Doreen come up for a breath. Doreen's head popped up. "How's it going?"

Doreen climbed back up, and into the cockpit. She was shivering. When she had wrapped a towel around herself and regained a normal breathing pattern she said, "I've only started to cut at it. I think we're in for a bad time with that plastic—it's heavyweight stuff—and I can only do a little bit before I have to come up. That water is colder than you think." Her skin had turned red from the cold, her lips blue.

"I'll go down next while you warm up. Give me the goggles." Veronica reached out and took them from Doreen, then removed her prosthetic leg. She picked up the knife.

"Then I can go down after she comes up. That way we each get a chance to thaw out for a while," said Ruby who was steering. In anticipation, Ruby pulled her long hair back and braided it tightly. The wind continued light, so the sloop kept sailing slowly toward its home port.

Veronica swung her leg over the stern, and dropped into the cold water. She was able to hack away another large section of plastic. Then up for air. Doreen and Ruby grabbed her arms and helped her to climb back aboard. The other two wrapped her in a big towel, knowing she'd need it. Her curly blonde hair hung down in salty dripping squiggles, and her teeth were chattering.

Ruby followed, then Doreen, and on and on and on. Over two hours passed. They worried about the person who was in the water, about sharks, about being unable to use the engine, about being stranded out there in the channel, about being run down by a freighter without the motor to pull them away. They were cold, wet, and miserable. Only their determination to free themselves kept them going.

Finally, Ruby's head burst out of the water. Before she even got back on board, she caught her breath and yelled, "It's clear!"

Doreen and her cousin swathed Ruby in towels, placing a cup of hot chocolate in her stiff icy fingers. Their relief immense, they celebrated by clanking mugs together and inventing a toast to their success. As soon as they had all changed into dry clothing, Doreen turned the ignition key. The engine sputtered to life. They had done it!

After a while the morning's playful mood returned. When they were closing up the boat that evening, they harmonized. "Row, row, row your boat, gently down the stream. Merrily, merrily, merrily, merrily, life is but a dream."

The wise person seizes on and savors peak moments of carefree joy, because lurking nearby may be tragedy. Within two days of the sailing trip, Ruby's husband Elliott has suffered a heart attack and is dead. Not many days after that, Veronica will be murdered.

20

Chapter 3

A few hours after Elliott Falstaff died, a blue Chevy van stopped at the Olive Canyon Resort gate. The driver reached out to punch the button that buzzed a doorbell in the office.

Dominic Pierce flipped the switch to open the heavy metal gate. He stepped over to the vehicle and smiled, saying, "Welcome to Olive Canyon. Please park there, and come into the office." He gestured at a nearby wide spot in the unpaved road.

Two minutes later a family of six joined Dom in the small concrete block room, stuffy in spite of two large oscillating fans. The windows revealed the blue van, blue sky, olive trees, dirt road, nothing more. Old olive trees were everywhere, the property having been used for olive crops for market long ago. The canyon rose sharply on three sides—the peaks to the west belonging to the Coastal Range of Southern California. As a nudist club location, the privacy afforded by the canyon was perfect.

Dom perched on the corner of his desk. The adults sat down on the folding chairs, and the children, ranging in age from three to ten, stood awkwardly behind their parents.

"I'm Dominic Pierce, the manager. Always glad to see new faces." His smile was genuine, even though it had a hard, brittle quality to it. His eyes could not smile this morning with Elliott Falstaff's demise so fresh in his memory. He wore only his athletic shoes. He had a hunch that this family would fit in beautifully at Olive Canyon, and be an asset to the club. They were obviously comfortable with Dominic's nudity, so he figured they were card-carrying sunbathers.

Introductions were completed. Dom said, "Here's Olive Canyon," indicating it on the large map tacked to the wall behind his desk. "We're here where the X is. This is our snack bar, open from 7 to 7 daily. Since it isn't run for profit, the prices are quite reasonable. Over here's the 105-degree Jacuzzi—it holds thirty adults comfortably, and is wonderful on a cool evening under the stars. It's off-limits to anyone under eighteen." Dom pointed to a square on the map. "Here's the recreation room where we hold several dances a year. Clothing is required, though—we hire live bands. These are campsites with all hookups, for those who wish to use a tent, trailer, or motor home. Several laundry, shower, and toilet buildings are scattered around our 200 acres. Here's our six night-lighted tennis courts, professional quality." Dominic stepped to the opposite side of the wall map. "Up here, about a mile to the west, is an outdoor chapel on a promontory with a great view. We hold sunrise services up there on Easter every year. Many folks who started coming here as single couples have been married there. Over here to the north we have a village of permanent trailer homes, mostly occupied by retirees." He paused, letting this information sink in as he stroked his full brown beard.

Dominic, having discovered that Joe Warner carried a valid ASA membership card, said, "Good. Then you already know the rules, but it's our policy to review them. We don't allow touching in public, except hand-holding. Staring is a no-no. Photography is out, so is getting drunk or using drugs. Beer is fine, if you stay sober. We even sell it in the snack bar. No one may wear clothing unless they have a good reason. Sunscreen, hats, shoes, and sunglasses are recommended. Always, but always, carry a towel to sit on, no matter where you sit. As you probably know, rule breakers are ejected, and blacklisted among all ASA camps."

While Dom talked, a shoving match erupted between the two youngest Warners, followed by stepping on each others' feet and giggling. Soon all four youngsters were wrestling around behind their parents' chairs. The mother's backward glance at them accompanied by a stage-whispered "Hush!" ended their shenanigans abruptly.

Grinning, realizing the children were getting restless, Dom hastened to complete his lecture with, "Our playground is well-equipped, but one of you should supervise. Here at Olive Canyon we encourage healthy outdoor activities: volleyball, tennis, swimming, diving, shuffleboard, and hiking. In poor weather we have an indoor heated pool, indoor games such as chess, billiards, checkers, ping pong, TV, computers, and video games. When your children are older they can join the Teen Club, and enjoy the company of their peers, supervised by an older teen that they choose themselves, with our approval of course. I know you'll enjoy our facilities, and I hope you'll return often."

As Joe handed the day's gate fee to Dominic, he said, "C'mon kids, let's go play." The children dashed out the door with the parents right behind them. The sun glistened on their shiny hair.

Alone in the office, Dom ran his hand over his high forehead, then down his neatly-trimmed, dark beard. *This has been quite a day, and it's only 11:30 in the morning.* His long bony face reflected weariness. *I can't get Elliott Falstaff's death off my mind. I hate thinking about it, but nudists die too.*

"Hi, honey. Gettin' hungry? It's almost lunchtime," Doreen said as she came in and flopped onto the chair where she had placed her towel. Her shoulder-length black hair was fastened up now into a bunch with a pink tie that matched her glasses' frames. Her only other clothing consisted of sandals, leaving her smoothly-tanned plump curves unfettered by clothing. She and her hubby looked like the illustrations in children's story books of Jack Spratt and his wife. Except these two were naked.

Dom replied, "Not yet. I haven't had a minute to think about food."

"That family that just came in? Cute little kids, aren't they."

"Yeah."

"Sometimes I wonder what our life would be like if things had been different, if our baby had survived. Don't you?"

The buzzer sounded its nerve-jangling *bzzz*. Another car at the gate.

"Back to work," he said, flipping the gate opener.

Doreen left to make lunch. If her husband happened to be too busy to join her in their quarters when the food was ready, she'd bring it to him in the office. Quite often, though, Howie Brill the gatekeeper would pop in and spell Dom at lunchtime.

While getting the food ready Doreen thought, *I try to please Dominic by doing nice things, like waiting on him when he's watching TV, and preparing special meals. But he never shows appreciation, or even says thanks. It's so depressing. I desperately need his love. Things started going downhill for us after we lost the baby. I've always believed he'll improve some day, but he's getting worse. Sometimes I think he wouldn't miss me if I drove off a cliff.* Her mind filled with last night's dream. She realized the same nightmare had haunted her off and on for months. In it she was struggling hard to run, straining as hard as she could, but her feet were stuck in black tar. She'd get one foot up a bit, but the other was stuck fast. She fought with all her strength to run away, but couldn't gain an inch. She was filled with panic, knew she had to get away—impossible! This scene repeated in her consciousness now, telling her something, but what?

Early in their marriage, through Dominic's love, Doreen developed positive feelings regarding her self, but felt very dependent on him. When she knew she was pregnant, Doreen quit attending college classes, so eager were they to have a healthy child.

Their daughter Claire arrived, a lovable child who looked much like Doreen with brown eyes and dark hair. Their joy was boundless until Claire succumbed to Sudden Infant Death Syndrome. They attended support-group meetings faithfully, and eventually recovered, as much as it's possible to recover from such a tragedy.

Doreen's girth hid a fragile personality. Eating chocolate bars was a form of solace—she became addicted to them. Weight gain was inevitable, but she just couldn't stop the chocolate intake. Dominic continued working and studying, becoming a certified public accountant. Doreen returned to classes, working part time with a clothing design firm. She started her own design company for the express purpose of creating clothing for overweight women like herself.

Doreen's business success amazed her. The days flew by, her creative juices pouring into everyday, business, and elegant clothing for large women. She hired a staff of competent employees, and frequently luxuriated in free time with her husband.

Dominic enjoyed a lucrative career, retiring at forty-eight after selling his business to a partner. His volunteer managerial position with Olive Canyon occupied only two days a week, a temporary situation until the club's accounts were in order.

Olive Canyon activities and sailing their sloop refreshed and relaxed them. Their primary residence, a modest Long Beach home, provided shelter when they were neither at Olive Canyon nor sleeping on the boat. At Olive Canyon they occupied the large, comfortable mobile home provided by the resort for its manager.

Chapter 4

The day after Elliott Falstaff's death, Dom rode his bike up the hill to Ruby's camper. She noticed the white cap above his tanned body as he parked his machine.

"Come on in, Dom," she called through the screen.

He did so, cap in hand, towel over his shoulder, staying just inside the door. The place was done in warm tones of peach and beige, very cozy looking.

"Sit down, Dominic, please," she said, gesturing toward a padded, upholstered booth with a Formica-topped fold-down table. He complied, settling onto his towel. He noticed her eyes were red and puffy.

"Ruby, Doreen suggested we could help you get this motor home back to the rental agency. I can drive it, and you and Doreen can follow in our car. Then we could drop you off at the Ontario airport for your flight home." He smoothed his beard, an old habit. "That's where you're leaving from, isn't it?"

She went to the refrigerator, put ice cubes into a glass, poured in lemonade, and handed it to him while saying, "Yes. But I don't want you to go out of your way for me. So much trouble." She stood at the sink, absently wiping the spotless counter.

"We're glad to be able to help in any way." He drank a bit of the cold liquid, admiring her coppery skin from beneath her long, graying, red hair all the way to her bare feet.

"You're too kind." She flashed an intoxicating smile.

Dom took another sip. *That's an odd way for a new widow to behave.* "It's settled then. What time does your plane leave?"

"At 1:45. I wasn't sure how I'd get this big bus returned to them. I guess I could drive it, but I'm just a little scared to try it. Elliott always did that." Her facial expression clouded momentarily, quickly regaining composure. Suddenly she wore a look of animal cunning, her dark eyes fastened on him.

He wondered if she had read his admiration.

She stepped closer, flipped her straight hair back, posing enticingly. Sensuously she murmured, "You're so sweet."

He ignored her obvious come-on. "Let's start out around nine tomorrow, so we won't have to worry about missing your flight, okay?" He had risen from his chair and scooped up the towel as he spoke. His hand flew to the screen door handle, while with the other hand he plopped his cap on his head.

He was opening the screen door when she sashayed closer, so her face was almost touching his, her bare nipples almost brushing his nude body, and said, "I can't tell you how much I appreciate this. I don't know how to thank you."

Departing hastily, Dom was speeding down the hill on his bike when he heard the door snap shut.

On Freeway 60 near Riverside, the gray Ford's driver pondered the complications of committing murder. *To act alone would be best; leave others out of it—the less anyone else knows the better. But how to go about it, how to kill this terrible woman, the destroyer of dreams? There was no other way justice would be served except by her death. But yes, I'll have to do it alone so no one else will be involved if I get caught. What if I get caught? Hadn't thought of that. I guess that's the chance I'll have to take. If I plan it right I won't get caught. I need a foolproof plan.*

CHAPTER 5

The morning sun rose to already-warm air, and Dom remembered they were planning to go sailing after taking Ruby to the airport. He showered and dressed in casual wear, feeling that familiar harnessed discomfort of clothing after being pleasantly nude for the past week. *This comfortable state becomes so natural after a while that a person ceases to observe whether another individual is clothed or not.* He recalled an incident when a woman was asking around the nudist camp if her friend had been in the coffee shop in the past hour. The cashier asked, "Was she wearing anything?" The woman replied, "I don't know—I didn't notice."

After breakfast they loaded sandwiches, apples, chocolate bars, cans of chilled 7-Up, and ice into their picnic cooler, putting it into the trunk of Dom's green three-year-old Buick.

Ruby, looking cool in a pale blue sleeveless seersucker dress, was waiting when they arrived. She handed the motor home's keys to Dom, who slid into the driver's seat of it and started the engine. Ruby climbed into the passenger seat of the still-running Buick. Doreen was behind the wheel with the air-conditioner on max. As soon as she started driving down the dirt road, Doreen pulled a chocolate bar from her huge purse. Offering it to Ruby, she said, "Have some of this? It'll make you feel better."

"No thanks. I had some toast just a little while ago."
Removing the paper from the sweets as she piloted
slowly along the bumpy lane, she asked. "You don't
mind if I munch, do you?"

"No. Go ahead." Ruby put on her sunglasses against
the glare.

When Dom parked the rented motor home in the lot of
U-DRIVE-'EM MOTOR HOMES Doreen and Ruby were
close behind in the Pierce's Buick. They transferred all of
Ruby and her late husband's luggage from the
Winnebago to the Buick's trunk.

Dom volunteered to drive, so Doreen slid out and sat
behind him for the short trip to Ontario Airport. Ruby
remained in the front passenger seat. Doreen fished
another chocolate bar out, offering it to the folks in front.
They declined, so she ate it all.

Waiting for her plane, Ruby seemed so alone and sad
that Doreen insisted they stay with her. Dom wondered
if Doreen would have felt the same degree of sympathy if
she were aware of Ruby's behavior toward Dom in the
motor home yesterday. While they loitered, they talked
mostly about neutral topics, although Ruby occasionally
referred to Elliott, and as she did so her eyes glistened
with tears. As Ruby started to go to the tunnel leading to
the plane, Doreen and Dom hugged her briefly, waved
goodbye, and left.

From there they drove to Long Beach to the
sailmaker's shop where they paid for and picked up the
new jib, then to the Long Beach Marina. *Windcatcher* was
bobbing gently in her slip, her halyard slapping
rhythmically on the aluminum mast. They climbed into
the cockpit. Dom unlocked the hatch, and slid it open,

dropping the new sail into the cabin below.

"I guess we won't have time to go to the Isthmus today. It's too late to start out now."

"Somehow I don't really feel much like it, do you?"

"No. Let's just sit here in the cockpit and have our picnic."

During the flight, Ruby Falstaff thought about arriving home in Indiana. Elliott's relatives had always treated her kindly, although she sensed their disapproval. Elliott had never told them that he and Ruby were sunbathers.

While chewing on her in-flight snack, Ruby decided to sell the house through a real estate broker, and move out of Indiana. Family ties, even her grown children, had ceased to interest her. She preferred to live in California.

Ruby's parents, both alcoholics, had moved frequently, their five youngsters changing schools and playmates often. Ruby's rebellious nature caused problems for her. She dropped out in tenth grade to marry Pierre Gireaux. The young couple moved to New Orleans where Pierre's family lived. Three children arrived in rapid succession to their father's great joy.

However, Ruby felt smothered by motherhood's responsibilities. Eventually she left her young family with their father, telling him she needed to see the world. Working as a maid on a luxury-cruise line, she traveled the oceans for several years, enraptured by the lure of foreign ports. Then she met Elliott Falstaff, whose attractiveness was only partly due to his airline-pilot position. Like Ruby, he was a rebel, introducing her to the sunbathers' world and to swinging. Their relationship began with the understanding that he was, and would continue to be, like the sailors, having women in every port. So whenever Elliott flew, Ruby welcomed the opportunity to experience other men, from whom she learned about marijuana, and numerous delights of the flesh. They called it an "open" marriage.

Chapter 6

The white catering truck—with Corrigan's Great Foods painted on the side in large red letters, accompanied by colorful pictures of sandwiches, coffee, ice cream treats, and sodas—was parked in its usual place at 11:55 a.m. In a few minutes when the noon whistles shrilled, the employees of the factories nearby would stream out to buy their lunches from Jake Corrigan.

Jake preferred a minimum of chit-chat with his customers, even the regulars who showed up at his truck every day. In conversations with family or friends, if he referred to those loyal folks who kept his business going, he'd say something like, "These suckers are as dependable as the noon whistle." His wavy dirty-blond hair and round clean-shaven face imparted a boyish look above his muscular frame. In his early forties, women found Jake's toothy grin attractive and thought he was much younger than he was.

His wife Veronica Corrigan—Doreen Pierce's cousin—serviced a different food route with a separate catering truck, supplying foods and beverages to another part of Riverside. She chatted with her customers, called them by name, and tossed out funny stories like a stand-up comedian. At thirty-nine her petite slim build, clear peach complexion, curly blonde hair, and deep-set blue eyes were admired by the men and envied by the women.

34

Her regulars looked forward to her comedy as the highlights of a dull workday.

They couldn't see that she had a prosthesis in place of her lower right leg, and sat on a high stool for comfort whenever she could. Injured in a terrible auto accident as a teenager, she had lost her leg but not her sense of humor.

Jake and Veronica had been members at Olive Canyon Nudist Resort for about a decade. Jake Corrigan, aggressive and competitive, enjoyed the volleyball games, while Veronica, a superior swimmer, preferred socializing in and around the pool and Jacuzzi because of her missing leg. Sometimes the Corrigans hired people to work the catering-truck routes for them and took a day or a week to relax at Olive Canyon, camping in their 32-foot Silver Streak travel trailer.

A few years back the Corrigans had purchased their home in Riverside. They installed a large heated pool and inflatable-dome cover soon after. Jake and Veronica and their acquaintances found the pool a perfect setting for their swinging activities. Minimal visibility due to the steam that rose from the warm water and swirled about—unable to escape the tightly-sealed translucent-plastic dome—added a modicum of privacy to the erotic ambience where couples and groups played adult games, groping about in the living embodiment of every young man's fantasy. Jake's prodigious penile endowment kept their swinging friends coming back for more, at the women's insistence.

Inside the house, a large picture of a nude painted on black velvet adorned their living room wall. It was one of those tawdry tasteless south-of-the-border bargains that

Jake had insisted they lug home with them from Tijuana, Mexico. A huge U-shaped, navy-velour sofa with several fluffy pillows dominated the room, lighted gently by two table lamps.

Months before Elliott Falstaff's fatal heart attack, Veronica and Jake were bare when their guests, the Pierces, entered. All the drapes were closed, and ceiling fans were silently circulating air. The room was cool, dark, and inviting.

Veronica said, gesturing toward the towel-covered sofa seats, "Make yourselves comfortable." This is the standard sunbathers' invitation to strip if guests so desire. The Pierces gladly shed their clothes.

Veronica said pleasantly, "Come on into the kitchen with me, Dory. I have a new cookbook I want you to see." The cousins vanished around the corner.

From behind the wet bar Jake asked, "What are you drinking, Dom?"

"The usual, please."

After handing Dom a Manhattan over ice, Jake sat across from him.

Jake asked, "Have you ever thought about swappin'?"

"Swapping?" Half Dom's drink went in a swallow. "You're kidding."

"Yeah, you with Veronica, and me with Doreen for about an hour."

"No. It's not for us. I hadn't ever thought about it."

"No shit? Brother, you just don't know what you're missin'. Believe me, Veronica's almost a nympho." Jake rolled his gray eyes meaningfully.

"No doubt a roll in the sheets with Veronica would be fun," he said, hoping to seem complimentary, "but I'd feel really strange, what with Doreen and Veronica being cousins." Dom gulped down the remainder of his drink, and reached for some pretzels.

"Yeah. A change of pace. Nothin' serious. Just fun and games." Jake was rolling a big unlit cigar around in his right hand, holding a gin and tonic in his left.

"After so many years with Doreen...I'd have to give that some thought."

Jake leered and asked, "How would you feel about me being with Doreen?"

"Uh, I don't know."

"Hey, good buddy, she deserves a change too." Jake stuffed a handful of potato chips in his mouth. "Everybody's gotta have some different stuff once in a while."

"Maybe so, but I don't think she'd be interested in swapping. She's pretty straight-laced. What would Veronica say about it?"

"No sweat." Jake flipped a match to life, holding it to his stogy while he sucked in great drafts until the thing was lit. He then expelled a cloud of noxious smoke. "Swingin's her favorite sport."

"I see." Dom's gaunt face became pensive. "In all these years we've known you two, we never even suspected." He chewed on a pretzel.

"We thought maybe you two were swingers cuz you're members of Olive Canyon like we are."

"Actually, Jake, we've been straight nudists for years, always playing by the American Sunbathers Association book. We didn't know you were swingers."

"We been swingers forever. I thought it was time you knew." Jake paused for a pull on his drink, then said,

"Swinging will improve your marriage."

"Is that so?" Dom grabbed another pretzel. "It's hard to believe we never knew about you two being swingers, never suspected. Doreen'll be shocked."

Jake got up and rummaged in a drawer of the lamp table. Handing Dom a business card, Jake said, "Here's the address in case you decide to check out the party scene. It's a BYOB cocktail party. Dress is casual, but most of the ladies wear their sexiest dresses." Rolling his eyes heavenward to emphasize his point he said, "Wait till you see 'em." Jake continued baiting the swing-party hook, detecting Dom's interest in spite of his protests. "You know, we have an open marriage like most swingers do. Once when Ronnie was gone to the mall, I called Cynthia Meissen to see if she was home. She was, and so was Ross. I told her I'd be right over. I grabbed my long coat and drove over to their house. I rang the doorbell. When she opened the door I flashed her—nuthin' under the coat, see? She laughed. I went in and the three of us had a good laugh over that. Then we had a great threesome. What fun! You just don't know what you're missin'."

Dominic nodded, thinking, *Maybe he's right. I don't know what I've been missing.*

"And another time when Ronnie and I were at Ed and Mona Lott's place, Mona wanted to just watch the action. She just had her hair done, and didn't want to get it messed up. So Ed and Ronnie and I just had ourselves a ball, several actually. Mona watched a while, then she got into it too—couldn't resist. Mussed up her hair, as I remember it, but we all had fun."

In the kitchen, as Veronica continued the dinner

preparations, she and Doreen were delighting in one another's company, feeling comfortable vibes. Doreen had always felt like she and Veronica were kindred spirits, joined by one of those extremely rare abilities to understand one another as if they had been Siamese twins. She sensed that her cousin Ronnie felt it too. Of course, she didn't know her cousin was a swinger.

While they chatted, Doreen helped Veronica put the foods into serving dishes. As soon as the meal was on the table Veronica poked her head around the corner, saying to the men, "Come on, you two. Dinner's ready."

On the way home, Dom thought about whether he should tell Doreen that the Corrigans were swingers. *I wonder if Veronica mentioned it. If Doreen doesn't bring up the subject I won't.* Doreen didn't mention it.

What do I know about killing someone? Hmm, not much I guess. I don't even like to watch murders on TV. But I've gotta do it. I will! She deserves to die, that's for sure. Maybe a time bomb would work.

CHAPTER 7

The following day, Olive Canyon sweltered in brilliant sunshine. Munching on a chocolate bar, Doreen plodded up the hill for a dip in the pool. The familiar scene awaited, humans of all ages wearing sandals or tennies, sunglasses, many sporting hats with visors or wide brims, nothing else. Tennis players, swimmers, divers, snack bar patrons, stretched-out sunbathers, volleyball players, shuffleboarders, children and toddlers—whose normal inclination is to be nude—playing games or chasing one another and squealing.

A sign near the pool read "Please shower first." The unisex shower room had six showerheads protruding from a thirty-foot tiled wall, with benches and towel hooks on the opposite wall between the six open windows. Two gray-haired men were chatting amiably under their side-by-side sprays. Doreen entered and parked her sandals under the bench, hanging her towel on a hook. She chose a spot near the men, turned on only the cold tap, wet down, then soaped. The man with the Mediterranean look was explaining that he and his family became sunbathers because they had lived next to a clothing-optional village on the shore of a lake in Eastern Europe, and found nakedness very agreeable in hot weather. The other man, pot-bellied and hairy, said he and his wife had been talked into it decades ago by close friends. Doreen remembered how she and Dominic unintentionally entered the social nudist lifestyle. They had been attending the same college, met and had become close friends. Fate stepped in—they fell in love. In a burst of spontaneity they drove one weekend to Las Vegas, found a justice of the peace, and married, returning to classes the following Monday.

During the summer of that year, their friends Shirley and Ron invited them to go to Olive Canyon Resort for a day. Not knowing it was a sunbathers' enclave, they packed a picnic, bathing suits and towels, and hopped into the other couple's car.

Arriving at the Olive Canyon gate, they were greeted by a nude gatekeeper. In the rear seat Doreen whispered to Dom, "Do you suppose this is a nudist colony?"

"Must be."

"What do we do now?"

"Let's just play along. I guess they thought we knew."

"Do I hafta take all my clothes off?"

"Guess so. Let's just have fun."

Shirley and Ron showed their membership cards and paid the gate fees. Driving up the hill to the parking lot, Doreen told them she had never been in a nudist camp before.

Shirley said, "You'll love it. After a few minutes you'll get used to it, and you'll hate putting clothes on when it's time to go home."

In the upper parking lot as soon as the car's engine stopped the two front doors burst open. Shirley and Ron jumped out, stripping rapidly, heaping clothing on the front seats. Dom and Doreen opened their doors hesitantly. Away to their left nude people of all ages and shapes were obviously having fun, in and around a pool whose clear water was as inviting as a carrot to a rabbit. The heat was intense, the water a magnet, and before they thought about modesty again, they were bare, having a wonderful time just like everyone else. They hated putting clothes on to go home.

After that surprising, exhilarating day they visited Olive Canyon often. Shirley and Ronald Decatur, their close pals, usually accompanied them.

The two men left the shower room. Doreen lingered under the cascading water a few minutes after the suds were gone. Then she slid into her sandals and sunglasses, grabbed her towel, and exited, still dripping, by the door nearest the pool.

Between the showers and the pool, a wide apron of concrete spread itself, extending to the area outside the snack bar. Umbrella-tables scattered there supported many cold drinks and foods. Numerous chairs held folks sitting on towels. As Doreen traversed the patio, she paused to greet friends, and returned the waves of a few people on the tree-shaded lawn that sloped uphill on the far side of the pool. *A typical summer day in the garden of Eden.*

Once inside the pool's chain-link fence, Doreen dropped her things in a pile, and jumped feet first into the deep end of the huge pool. *Ahh, that feels good.* As her head shot up out of the water she grabbed the molded concrete edge. The chaise lounges were placed so that people could sit up and watch the pool's activities, their foot ends being next to the water. Veronica occupied the lounge facing Doreen.

"Hi, Ronnie. I didn't see you folks come in today."

Veronica Corrigan lifted her lacy white hat, raised her

head, and said, "Dory. Good to see you." Her face lit up. "We came in early. You must have been busy."

Doreen climbed out of the pool, retrieved her towel, sunglasses, and sandals, and sat on her towel on the concrete next to Veronica's chaise lounge. Veronica pulled herself up to perch on the edge of it, rubbing the stump below her right knee in a subconscious way, more from reflex than from real itch. Her prosthesis lay next to her like a precious doll.

"Do you have any plans for this evening?" Veronica asked.

"None that I know of."

"We're having a few friends come to our house later, around nine, for a swim. We'd like to have you and Dominic join us."

"Sounds terrific. I'll ask Dom, and let you know." She stood up.

Veronica flipped up the cap of her lotion, and squirted a big blob onto her palm. "I hope you can make it. We'd love to have you visit."

Doreen recognized the sincerity of her cousin's statement, enjoying the warm glow of a special mutual relationship.

"We'll be there, most likely. Thanks for inviting us." She turned and headed down the hill to ask her husband if he felt like putting on clothing in order to leave Olive Canyon that evening to visit the Corrigans. Sometimes that was asking too much in hot weather.

Veronica had stretched out again, and was rubbing lotion all over her nude body. All around the pool naked folks were relaxed and content like lizards baking in the sun. Several had aged and wrinkled flesh, a few had surgical scars, many were overweight or underweight, but none displayed the classical "beauty pageant" image—they were humans, after all, with their human flaws.

"Dom, guess who I just met by the pool—Ronnie." Doreen met him on the path between the office and the mobile home.

"So what's new?" he asked, following her inside.

"She invited us to their house this evening. Seems they're having some friends over for a swim. Wanna go?" She started getting things out of the refrigerator to make sandwiches.

He washed his hands, then watched her retrieve four slices of bread from the whole wheat loaf. "Sure. Why not? It might be fun."

After lunch Dom returned to the office. Doreen scrutinized her wardrobe, studying each dress, realizing that most of her clothes were at their own home in Long Beach. *I'll dress up a bit tonight. Maybe those friends aren't nudists. This soft yellow silk hides my excess weight better than the others—but I'll have to wear a bra. God, how I hate those things, binding my ribs and riding up.* The decision made, she helped herself to a chocolate bar in the kitchen.

Hours later when Dom and Doreen climbed out of their sedan across the street from the Corrigan's home in Riverside, it was almost dusk. The sprawling Mission-style stucco had a small front lawn with palm trees and shrubs enhanced by hidden lighting. Their two catering vans sat side by side on the driveway. Approaching the door, they could hear laughter and music.

The doorbell's chimes brought Jake, who said, "Come on in. Glad you could join us." He was wearing a gray knit shirt with navy slacks. Doreen thought, suppressing a giggle, *It's so seldom I see him with clothes on—very nice.* Jake's wavy hair and bulging muscles added to his attractiveness. She knew he could be a smooth-talking charmer with women when he wanted. With men, he was a cigar-chewing macho type.

The others were having drinks outside on the patio.

Jake asked, "Having the usual?" then prepared refreshments for the Pierces.

As soon as Dom, Doreen, and Jake stepped out through the sliding glass door, Veronica started to introduce the other couple, Cynthia and Ross Meissen, but Doreen said, "We've met at Olive Canyon. Hi, Cynthia and Ross, and you too, Ronnie."

For a while the three couples chatted, swapping jokes and stories, drank, and munched on chips and dip. Doreen was amazed at how different Cynthia and Ross Meissen looked and behaved this evening, compared to their composure at Olive Canyon. *Much looser, must be the alcohol.* They sat close, often touching one another in ways that were forbidden at the resort. Doreen particularly liked the way they exchanged loving glances. *Dom and I haven't done that since we were first married.* She knew the Meissens had three children in their teens, having seen them at the nudist resort. They had a small business of some sort, something to do with boats, and they lived near the business in San Pedro.

Cynthia and Ross appeared to be to be around forty. Ross was the type of blond who tanned nicely, but a little spare tire pushed at the buttons of his Hawaiian print shirt. Cynthia looked Italian: olive complexion, classic facial features, and wavy dark brown hair. She was

45

pleasingly plump, a Rubens painting in the flesh. Her slinky black, low-cut dress was very revealing, also very flattering—Doreen envied her.

Veronica the joke teller asked, "Didja hear about the two old women at the nudist park? They were just sitting on a bench talking when an old man streaked past. One woman asked the other, 'What was that?' The other said, 'I'm not sure, but it needed ironing pretty bad.'"

As the chuckles subsided Doreen studied the huge green translucent plastic dome hiding the swimming pool—the combination of lights inside and vapor rising off the warm water and swirling around, trapped inside the dome, made an eerie revolving greenish glow.

"That thing looks like something from another planet," Doreen said, indicating the great green bubble.

"It's just wonderful in there, all warm and steamy," said Cynthia. "As soon as I finish this drink I'm going in."

Doreen said, "Since Veronica told us there would be other people over for a swim, and we didn't know if they were nudists or not, we brought our towels and swim suits."

Cynthia gave a loud snort and shouted, "Swimsuits! Don't expect me to wear one! I hate 'em."

The outburst caught everyone's attention. Cynthia jumped up, unzipped her frock, and kicked off her shoes, yelling, "Last one in is a toad!" She had worn nothing under the dress.

Soon clothing was being shed like snakeskin, bare bodies disappearing into the green dome. Dom and Doreen were the last ones to enter.

"This is different from what I expected this evening. Fun though," Doreen whispered to Dom. "I'm glad we're all nudists. I'm so used to the nice feeling of the water on my skin."

Dom thought, *I bet Ross and Cynthia are swingers too. I guess Doreen will find out about it tonight.*

All the lights were underwater, installed in the sides of the pool. The mist rising from the warm water made it difficult to see more than a few feet, and pitiably nearsighted Doreen, her glasses off because of steaming up, was nearly sightless. Squinting, she kept a hand on the side of the pool so she could feel where she was, walking ahead until the water was up to her neck.

Soon Jake swam up close to her, his hand landing on her left breast as he stood up next to her. Doreen moved out of his way, thinking he probably hadn't been able to see her while he was underwater.

Jake said, "Come 'ere baby. I love big tits—they turn me on."

Doreen, horrified, backed into shallower water, trying to ignore him, but he followed. *I wonder if Ronnie knows he's like this.* She turned and pushed through the water toward the shallow part as fast as she could, with Jake patting her retreating derriere. She hurried up the steps and wrapped herself in a towel. He turned and swam away.

Meanwhile, in the dim light Veronica studied Dominic. *He's like Abraham Lincoln with less hair. He's so thin and tall, with those piercing eyes, and that beard too.* She waded over until she was next to him, dove under, then ran her fingers gently along the inside of his thigh. He jumped, surprised, and looked down expecting to find Doreen there. At that moment Veronica swooshed up out of the water, her face against his chest.

"Like that?" she asked teasingly, her fingers making circles on his abdomen.

"Yes. But..." He suddenly ducked and swam away. As he stood up he noticed Doreen huddling in her towel.

"Had enough?" he asked. "Are you cold?"

"Yes to both questions," she answered curtly.

Grabbing his towel Dom called into the rolling fog, "We have to get back to Olive Canyon now. Thanks for the hospitality. Good night, all. We'll find our way out."

As they were closing the dome's door they heard Jake saying, "Come again," then Cynthia squealing, "I'm coming now!"

Doreen and Dominic dried and dressed for the drive home. Carrying their damp towels, they were heading for the Buick, out the side gate and down the concrete that fronted the double garage.

"Dom, listen!" She stopped walking. "Why would something be ticking in one of the lunch vans? I've never heard them do that before." She cocked her head toward the sound coming from the catering van.

Dom stopped, moved closer to the van and said, "I hear it too. A definite ticking."

"I think I'll just go back and let them know about it. Maybe it's something they need to look into."

"Go ahead. I'll wait here."

Doreen trotted back to the green-domed pool, and entered the cover. "Veronica! Veronica! One of your trucks out front is making a ticking sound. Is that okay?"

"What? That doesn't seem right. I've never heard any ticking in either of the trucks." Veronica hurried out of the pool, followed by Jake, and then the Meissens. After wrapping in a towel and getting her prosthetic leg,

Veronica rushed to the front of the house. Jake and the others were close behind.

As soon as Veronica saw Dominic near the truck she asked, "What do you suppose it is?"

"No idea. Never heard anything like it before."

Jake yelled, "Don't touch it. Maybe it's a bomb! I'm calling the cops," and ran in the front door.

CHAPTER 8

"He's right. Let's all get inside." Doreen shouted, following Jake into the house. "Better safe than sorry."

As soon as they were safely in the house, Veronica said, "Let's go get our clothes on before the cops arrive."

A squad car screamed into the street in five minutes, red lights pulsating. Jake rushed out. The siren died with a groan, and two uniformed men jumped out. Running to the vehicle Jake indicated, they listened to the ticking, nodding at one another. "This one's for the explosives guys," and radioed that message to headquarters. Yellow caution tape quickly cordoned the vicinity, and onlookers were shooed away. Jake, his wife, and his guests went behind the house as ordered.

The bomb squad arrived shortly after the radio call. Clad in thick heavy protective gear and using special equipment, they slithered gingerly into and under and around the van. Locating the source of the ticking wasn't difficult. Disarming it took a little longer.

The back yard group waited anxiously for a report from the crew in the driveway. Conversation was minimal—each could focus on only one topic, the bomb. Speculation was useless. After several attempts to lighten the moment fell flat, no one else spoke. Even Veronica couldn't tell one of her jokes.

Eventually, they heard the quick footsteps of an officer coming around the corner. They sat up, all attention on the man. "We got it! You can relax now."

"What a relief! Was it a time bomb?"

"Yup. Set to detonate at noon tomorrow." Grim faced, he said, "The amount of explosive material would have blown you, the truck, and anyone nearby into the next county." His arms flew into the air.

"That's my truck," Veronica said, jumping up. "It would have exploded tomorrow when I'd be selling to the lunchtime crowd at one of the factories. My God!" Legs weak, she sat down hard, weeping. Doreen held her hand. Anger and confusion muddled their thoughts.

Grilling by the police produced no answers as to who or why the bomb.

Jake and Veronica were puzzled. Jake said, "It was likely meant for me, not Veronica. I'm kinda hardnosed about things sometimes. Prob'ly made some enemies. But everybody likes Veronica."

At Olive Canyon Eatery, a cafeteria with two long walls of screened windows, its end-to-end tables and benches half filled, the chatter of patrons droned. Surrounded by other naked people having lunch, a young woman and her little daughter were eating grilled cheese sandwiches and drinking milk, seated on towels at one of the picnic tables. A very tiny baby lay sleeping in its blue-blanket-lined carrier on the table next to them. The infant first squirmed, then screwed up its face, and then let out a few shrill squawks, drawing amused glances from the other patrons who understood from the sounds that this one was only a few weeks old. The three-year-old spoke softly to her baby brother, "Don't cwy, don't cwy." Her mother scooped up the diaper-clad noise-maker, putting him to her unclothed breast, where he suckled contentedly. Quiet returned.

Twenty-two year-old Ashley West watched from the opposite side of the table. Her spouse Smokey, a rangy fellow with long dirty-blond straggly hair, sat beside her chewing on his cheeseburger, seeing but not noticing, lost in his own world. His real name was Derek. However, Smokey was more appropriate since he had been a heavy pot-smoker for many years. Although drug use was forbidden at the resort, he often went to their pickup camper for a hit, burning incense to cover the marijuana.

Jake Corrigan moved away from the cash register, carrying his tray of food. Looking around for familiar faces, he chose the vacant spot next to Ashley and Smokey.

"Hi. How ya doin'?" he asked as he set down his lunch, then his towel, then himself.

Ashley's freckly face curved into a smile as she munched her cheeseburger. "Great." A lock of red-gold hair fell in her eyes.

Smokey said, "What's new?"

"Not much," Jake said, piling ketchup and relish on his hamburger.

An hour later Ashley, Smokey, and Jake sat around drinking beer in the West's camper under the olive trees, at the farthest campsite up the hill and to the north. The camper's tiny windows were open, but still the place smelled stuffy and smoky. An incense candle burned on the minuscule table.

"Some more?" Smokey offered a lit joint to Jake.

"Sure," Taking it between thumb and forefinger, he sucked on it until his lungs were full, holding the smoke as long as possible before expelling it slowly, passing the joint to Ashley. "Ahhh, good shit," he exclaimed, chasing it with a slug of cold beer.

Ashley took a toke in the same way, and passed the paper-wrapped pot along to Smokey, saying, "I'm stoned. Way out. How about you?"

"Yeah, me too. I'm gettin' the munchies," Smokey said.

Jake took another hit. "I'm gettin' the hornies. This here's a mighty nice little rig—I see you got a big bed up there. Room for three?"

"Why not? I got the hornies too," Ashley said, gulping her beer and hopping into the bed after another hit.

Kicking off their flip-flops, Jake and Smokey jumped in with her.

Nothing in the paper about the bomb killing her. I guess I'd have heard by now if it got her. Maybe I should buy a gun, one of those stolen ones that can't be traced, and a silencer for it. But when could I use it, and where? Maybe some night when she's alone in the dark. Sure, when would that be, her with a husband. Maybe a gun's too quick, maybe I oughta make her suffer before I kill her. No, bad idea. Maybe I could pay someone else to kill her for me, like a hit man. I could say," Just do it and get it over with."

CHAPTER 9

At Olive Canyon Nudist Resort, the late morning air from the open windows stirred the smell of freshly-made coffee through the mobile home.

Taking two mugs off their hooks, Doreen asked, "What did you think of the Corrigans' pool party?"

Warily Dom replied, "What do you mean?"

Pouring the coffee, she said, "Did you have a nice time in their pool?"

Taking the cup that Doreen handed him, he said, "It's time you knew, if you haven't figured it out already. They're swingers."

"Really?" She scowled briefly. "That explains why Jake got fresh with me in the pool. How is it we didn't know? Ronnie never told me."

"What did he do to you?"

"Nothing much, really. He put his hand on my boob and said big tits turn him on. That's when I got out of the water."

Dom grinned. "Veronica came on to me like a piranha. That's when I got out, too. Although I must admit, she's a temptation, that's for sure."

"I'm not interested in being a swinger, Dom." Talking quietly, she was trying her best to hide how upset she was.

"Those swing parties Jake's been telling me about sound pretty interesting."

"Really?" His enthusiasm frightened her since she

always felt her security threatened when Dom expressed even the most innocent interest in other women.

"Jake says Veronica loves those parties as much as he does."

"Ronnie, my cousin Ronnie does? She's never mentioned them to me."

"Yes. He said they've been swingers since before they married each other."

"That's fine for her, for them. But not for me. I never knew about them."

"I'd like to go to one of those party houses Jake told me about."

"You mean that? You're serious?" She unwrapped a chocolate bar and devoured it nervously.

"Why not? Please, Dory, think of it as recreational sex. Besides, I wouldn't go to a party to participate. Only to look around, see what it's like, satisfy my curiosity."

"But I don't want to have anything to do with other men. Just you."

"Come on. It's not serious, just fun and games." Dom scrubbed through his beard with his fingertips, raking it downward.

"I have to admit I'm kinda curious to see what a party house is like. But I would definitely stay away from the bedrooms—no one would have to know I'm not participating in the sex. They wouldn't necessarily know, would they?"

"They'll all be busy—probably no one will know. How could they?" He took a sip from his coffee, and added, "Doreen, you know the difference between love and lust. The parties are intended for lust only, no love involved."

"Honey, I don't want to be a swinger. Screwing around with other men goes against everything I've ever believed." She took a swallow of coffee and a bite of chocolate, then another and another, chewing fast.

"I can understand that. But I really would like to see what the parties are like someday. Just give it a try. Once."

"Let me think about this for a while. I admit it, I am a bit curious."

That's it, that's it! It'll work, I know it. She goes out there alone in the pool lotsa times. She won't even know I'm there, so she won't yell or scream. She won't even be able to put up much of a fight—she's such a lightweight, and only one good leg to stand on. It'll be easy to hold her head under for a coupla minutes. Nothin' to it.

CHAPTER 10

The next day Dom figured that since Doreen had said she was curious about the swing parties, she might be ready to attend one. *Strike while the iron's hot*, he thought. Casually bringing up the topic once more, he revealed to his wife more of what Jake had said. Again he asked her to accompany him to one of the couples-only affairs, hinting that if she refused, he would find some other willing partner.

Assuming he would invite someone else in her place, Doreen said, "If it means so much to you, I'll go." Then, after hesitating, "Will you be with other women?"

"I don't know. You know I've never been a ladies' man, so I doubt it."

"Okay, let's go to one. Guess I'm just nosy. I'd like to see what goes on at a swing party, and how the house looks, and all." Doreen went to her closet, began pawing through dresses. "What should I wear?"

"Jake says some of the women get all gussied up in sexy dresses, but not all of them. Why not wear something dressy that you're comfortable in?"

"Good idea."

I hope everything goes the way I planned. Then no one will ever be able to find out who killed her. It's a great idea, if I do say so myself. Revenge is sweet, and I'm about to taste it tonight.

Many cars were parked on both sides of the pleasant, tree-lined street with its handsome homes. Doreen checked the house number of a large two-story white Colonial and said, "This is the place," to Dominic. Doreen's palms were sweaty with anxiety—they were about to attend their first swing party. She thought, *I need another Hershey bar.* She refrained. She had gobbled two of them during the thirty minute drive from home.

It was dusk as the Pierces entered the building. A large almost-prissy older man greeted them, collecting the fees at an elegant marble-topped table in the vestibule.

"Hello. I'm Elmore May." In the dim light his jowly face with its neat mustache appeared jovial as he stood up and extended his right hand. His thick glasses failed to hide laugh-lines around his green eyes.

"Hello," Dom said, smiling and reaching to shake hands. "We're the Pierces. I called you this morning."

"Yes, I recall. You're friends of Jake and Veronica Corrigan."

"Right," Dom said. "They told us about the parties. Doreen and Veronica are cousins."

"The Corrigans just got here a few minutes ago." Elmore stuck his hand out again. "It's twenty dollars for tonight. By the way, we don't allow any nudity, lewd behavior or obvious activities, except in the bedrooms, of course. Agreed?"

"Sure. Here you are," Dom said, handing him the cash.

"Have fun." Elmore sat down, shoving the bill into his pocket.

In a softly-lit room directly ahead of them several nicely dressed people sat on easy chairs, loveseats, and sofas, talking, snacking, and sipping. Dom and Doreen recognized all of them from Olive Canyon. A few steps to the left a bright kitchen beckoned. To the right a darkened hallway opened onto many unlit rooms. They could see the lower part of a night-lighted stairway going up to the floor above.

Dom and Doreen went to the kitchen. A slate-gray tile counter came into view, loaded with ice-buckets, clean glasses, mixes, sodas, pretzels, chips, and cookies, as well as bottles of gin, bourbon, Scotch, and several others. All had their owners' names marked on them. They found Veronica and Jake mixing gin-and-tonics.

"Hi. I'm glad to see you decided to try it," Veronica said, picking up her glass and moving away from the counter. Doreen thought, *Veronica looks lovely, and many years younger than her true age of thirty-nine. Even the lower leg prosthesis takes nothing from her overall attractiveness.*

"Hi, Ronnie," Doreen said. "Good to see you. You too, Jake."

"Hi, Dom. Hi, Dory," Jake said. Close to his wife's head he whispered, "Meet me in the living room at midnight. I'm off to have some fun." He flicked his tongue into her ear and strode away grinning, drink in hand. Veronica giggled a little and headed for the living room.

Doreen dropped ice into two glasses, poured 7-Up in hers, and bourbon and 7 in Dom's. They joined the others.

Veronica had settled onto a loveseat where Dom joined her, beginning a quiet conversation. Doreen perched on the end of a vacant sofa and glanced around, becoming very unhappy. She felt like an overdressed cow—several of the other women wore lace-and-satin mini-mini outfits designed to attract a man's attention. She could talk with no one, unless she pushed herself into the company of cozily chatting couples. Dark-haired Barbara Sweet, in the purple satin dress, snuggling with nice-looking Ross Meissen in the blue shirt, surely didn't want Doreen butting in. Ed Lott, a tall man of medium build with carefully manicured hair, and attractive Cynthia Meissen, in black lace, arose and left. The other couples weren't seeking Doreen's company either.

Doreen felt left out, ignored. She took chocolate from her purse and nibbled on it.

I came here to see this house, so that's just what I'll do. Maybe that'll make me feel better. At least I'll have something to do. She put her drink down, picked up her purse, and left the room. Tiptoeing along the plushly-carpeted, dark corridor she glanced into the rooms, of which several were bathrooms with huge stacks of clean folded towels. Still chewing on chocolate, Doreen found a bedroom that seemed empty; nothing on the clothes hooks on the wall. A couple of feet ahead, stretching across the room from side to side, hung hospital privacy curtains that blocked her view. The drapes were on tracks so she cautiously pushed one aside. Curiosity drove her in. Lighted only by a tiny nightlight, the door-less room was partitioned into halves by the hanging curtains, with a sheet-covered mattress on each half of the carpeted floor.

Returning to the hallway, she heard heavy breathing and moans of pleasure coming from the next room down the hall. She thought, *Even though they can't see each other, those noises must be quite a turn-on to the people on the other mattress in that room.* She felt strange hearing their sexual activity, as if she shouldn't be listening. A blush heated her shoulders, neck, and face. Even so, she couldn't tear herself away. When another couple in the room began to make similar sounds, she moved on thinking, *This place is incredible. Where's Dom when I need him?*

She crept quietly up the stairs. Outside a bedroom she thought she heard Dom's deep resonant voice, so she hurried on, feeling extremely nervous. Knowing Dom was with another woman was more upsetting than she had imagined it would be. She felt betrayed, and foolish for coming here.

I've got to kill her tonight, here, soon. I may never get another chance as good as this. Everyone's busy, no one's watching. I'm sure she'll come out alone for a swim—she does every week. I'll just stay out by the pool where it's real dark and no one can see me. When she gets in the water and starts to swim, I'll slip in behind her like a shark on the prowl. It'll be so easy, so quick. She'll never even know what happened.

Down the hall, Doreen read the sign above the door: GROUP ROOM. *This room's different, no privacy curtains. The one dim nightlight in there does as much good as a candle in a mine.* Sheet-covered mattresses hid the entire floor. About five or six nude people in an orgy of foreplay and sensuality—hands caressing, tongues titillating, pleasuring women and men indiscriminately, everyone giving and receiving—were absorbed in their fun while she watched. Each person's libido was expressing itself lovingly, innocently, openly, without guile or pretense, like children at play. At first she was embarrassed, standing in the doorway as she was, then she realized that they were either so preoccupied that they unaware of her, or they truly didn't care who saw them. Soft ahs and mmms of pleasure reached Doreen's ears. After several minutes she became aware that no sexual intercourse was taking place.

Lust only, Dom said. Damn! That looks like it might be fun. Suddenly, like the final curtain dropping, a barricade of ugly inhibitions filled Doreen's mind. Gone was the innocence. She quickly left.

About 10:30, Doreen, having wandered throughout the entire large house, returned to the living room. Dom was there, dressed and alone, looking bored.

"How'd it go, honey?" she asked.

"Okay." He perked up, seeing her. "How about you? Have fun?"

"It was all right." She sat next to him. "I watched a bunch of people in the group room. They all turned each other on."

"Veronica went off with someone else. Then Cynthia practically dragged me upstairs, but I couldn't get interested in her, a total flop. Not my type, I guess."

Relieved, Doreen said firmly, "Dom, I've had enough of this swinging stuff, and I hope you have too."

He grinned. "At least now we know firsthand what it's like."

Doreen assumed this meant he'd also had enough. She reached for Dominic's hand. "Have you seen what's out back?"

"No. Let's take a look before we go home."

Behind the house darkness reigned. The only illumination came from ground-level low-wattage lamps around the perimeter of the swimming pool, placed three feet back from the edge to give the utmost privacy to those in the water. Located about forty feet behind the house, the slick surface of the water was black and shiny, reflecting the sky. Chaise lounges, tables, chairs, and shrubbery showed themselves in shadowy form to Doreen and Dom when their eyes adjusted to the darkness. They sauntered hand in hand toward the pool.

"Look! Something's sticking out from under that dark lump."

"It looks like my cousin's—" Doreen said, picking something up. "Ronnie's prosthesis, her leg! Where's Ronnie?" She cried out, "Ronnie, Ronnie, are you here?"

"She wouldn't have gone into the house without that, would she?"

"No, she couldn't, unless she crawled." In a panicky voice, "Where *is* she?"

Chapter 11

They scoured the entire fenced area in back of the house. No Veronica.

Doreen felt shaky, wanted to scream.

Dom found a switch that controlled floodlights. He joined Doreen peering into the depths of the pool.

Nothing but frustrating blackness.

Doreen, holding down the panic she felt, ran to the manager, asked for a flashlight, or pool lights, telling him the problem.

Elmore flicked on lights that were embedded in the sides of the pool below the water line. The three of them crouched on their hands and knees at the pool's edge.

Hoping to find nothing. Dreading what they might see.

Doreen screamed, "There!"

From the hazy bottom at the deep end, Veronica stared up through sightless eyes.

Dominic and Doreen jumped in, clothes and all.

Elmore's face was gray putty. He said, "I'll call the paramedics," and ran toward the house.

The chlorinated water stung Doreen's eyes. She frantically struggled to see or feel her cousin. Unbearable tension gripped her as seconds ticked by. She was desperate by the time she saw the pale ghostly figure on the bottom.

Dom also located Veronica. They each grasped an

arm, and fought through the water with every bit of strength they could command. Finally they surfaced. The breath they'd been holding blasted out. Gasping, they sucked in as much air as possible.

"Is she alive?" Tears came to Doreen's eyes, although she fought to hold them back.

"Don't know yet."

Together they quickly laid Veronica on the concrete and turned her head to one side. Dom straddled her body and began rhythmic pressure to her chest. Doreen held Veronica's nose and blew air into her lungs between pushes. Since Veronica had been in ninety-degree water, her skin was warm to touch, holding out the hope of life.

People trickled out of the house to watch and whisper, having heard the scream.

Soon paramedics rushed to Veronica's side with equipment. "We'll take it from here," one of them said.

The Pierces jumped up and out of the way.

"This is awful. Someone has to tell Jake." Dory couldn't take her eyes off Ronnie.

"I'll tell him." Looking pale and grim, he turned away, and left Doreen sobbing.

It took a little while for Dominic to find Jake, peering into one dark room after another, and listening for Jake's voice. As soon as Dom told him about Veronica, Jake grabbed his clothing and raced out of the house.

He stayed as close to his wife as allowed, his eyes glued to the rescue efforts. After a time that seemed forever, the men working on Veronica shook their heads, and the life-saving battle was abandoned. One of them brought a gurney on which they placed the body. They loaded her into the ambulance and left, after obtaining the information they needed.

Two police officers arrived, a woman and a man. The rooms became bright, as they searched for evidence of foul play, finding only Veronica's clothes in a bathroom where she had changed for her swim.

Jake's macho facade had disappeared—he was incredulous and shocked as he slumped on a sofa. "I can't believe it. She's such a live wire." He brushed at the tears that kept coming.

Doreen sat weeping on Jake's left, trying to find words to comfort him. In an easy chair, Dom remained stoic, swathed in towels, barefooted, his wet clothing and shoes in a plastic grocery bag at his feet.

When Ruby entered the room, the Pierces were amazed—they hadn't known she was at the party. She went to Jake, who was wiping his eyes, and squeezed in on his right side on the sofa.

Veronica had been popular—most of the women wept. Dick Weiner brushed tears away too. Jake and Ruby took turns using Jake's big white handkerchief.

The policewoman was about thirty-five, medium height and sturdily built, with short reddish-brown hair peeking from beneath her cap. A serious no-nonsense face with premature wrinkling and blue-gray eyes turned toward Jake as she strode over to him.

"I understand you're the victim's husband?" she asked Jake, who was still on the sofa. "Are you able to answer a few questions?"

"I'm okay." Jake sniffled.

"Did your wife ever swim alone?" The officer's face appeared sympathetic but her eyes were hard.

"Often. She told me that she liked to swim between

encounters, and preferred to be by herself." His eyes and nose were red now, but the tears had stopped.

"Had she been drinking?"

"Yes. She had a gin and tonic when we arrived, and I don't know if she had more drinks after that. I wasn't with her."

A look of disgust washed the officer's countenance as she said, "I see. Did she sometimes drink too much at these parties?"

"Sometimes she had as many as three very light ones, I think. But no, she never got drunk, if that's what you mean."

"Yes, thank you, Mr. Corrigan. That's it for now. Sorry about your wife's accident."

Just then several plain-clothes officers arrived with their equipment and went to work. When they were satisfied, they allowed the swingers to go, after cautioning them not to take any out-of-town trips right away, since they might be needed to answer questions.

On the way home Doreen said, "What an evening! Our first and last swing party, and we lost Ronnie. I still can't believe it." She unwrapped a chocolate bar, and took a bite after offering it to Dominic. Tears slid down her cheeks, then she just gave in and wept silently. Suddenly anguished moans came from deep within, her body heaving in grief. "I loved her. We weren't just cousins, we were soul mates."

"It's awful." He paused in thought. "I wonder how Jake will manage."

In a flash of insight, Doreen, who had expected to be comforted by her husband, now realized that he was more concerned about Jake than he was about her. She recalled other times when Dom seemed uncaring. The awful truth began forcing its way into her consciousness: he really doesn't care about me. *I'm just his wife, a habit, nothing more.* She quickly buried that thought, and turned her attention to Veronica's death.

As the Buick purred down the freeway, Doreen said, "The more I think about it, the more I think her death wasn't an accident. She was a really strong swimmer. Her upper body was powerful. She'd been compensating with her arms for the loss of that leg since she was in her teens. What do you think?" She gobbled a chocolate bar.

"I'm inclined to believe it was an accident. Although it's true, she never seemed to be affected much by gin." He smoothed his beard down, his brows furrowed.

"Who could possibly want to see Veronica dead?"

"What are you raving about, Doreen? It was an accident."

"Do you suppose we should do some discreet snooping on our own?" Doreen chewed on another big bite of chocolate. "Let's make it a point to socialize more with the partygoers when they show up at Olive Canyon. But we'll have to be careful not to make anyone suspicious."

Dom patted his beard down, a habit denoting concentration. "Let the police do what they will. You keep your nose out of it."

"But, honey, I'm sure we could find out a lot more at Olive Canyon than the police could." She finished the candy and wadded the paper into the plastic trash container hanging from the dash.

"There's nothing to find out. It was an accident, plain and simple."

Doreen was disappointed at his attitude, and thought, *I'll dig into my cousin's murder some more, whether he likes it or not.*

As if he could read her thoughts, he said, "Doreen, don't try to be a detective. It was just an accident—tragic to be sure, but still an accident."

"But Ronnie was my *cousin* and your *friend*, doesn't that mean anything? And what if they keep on believing it was an accident? They'd never look into it." Her voice became shrill. She slid closer to the car door in annoyance. *After all, how dangerous can it be, talking to friends?*

His tone was brusque, "Keep out of it!" He glanced at her. She was staring fixedly out the window. He shouted, "Do you hear me, Doreen? I'm ordering you to mind your own business."

In the ensuing silence, Doreen huddled in the car seat as far away from Dom as possible. *That man, Avery Trent, Ruby brought to the party—twenty years her junior—who is he? Ruby and Jake were chummy before Ruby's husband Elliott passed away. The two couples played billiards and tennis at the Resort. What's their relationship now? I better quit thinking about it, Dom's really mad at me.* She said nothing more about her suspicions that evening.

Sitting alone in the dark living room for a long time, the murderer thought, *I should be feeling pleased with myself, but I'm not. I'm miserable, worried about getting caught. It didn't go the way I'd figured it would. The plan seemed so cut-and-dried, but now I'm not so sure I did the right thing. She's dead, true, my revenge is accomplished. I never killed anything before, not anything, even bugs. It was much harder than I ever figured it would be, holding her head underwater till she stopped fighting. She was a lot stronger than I thought she'd be. Even though she had only one leg to stand on—it wasn't hard to sweep her off it from behind—she put up quite a fight. No, not at all the way I figured it would go.*

CHAPTER 12

Doreen was busy in one of the nudist resort's laundry rooms when Ruby Falstaff wheeled in her cartload of dirty clothes saying, "My washer's on the blink at my apartment, so I brought 'em with me." They greeted with a hug.

"That's a pretty shirt, Ruby. Pink's a nice color on you."

"Thanks. I was cool this morning, what with it overcast today, so I decided to wear this shirt and these old slacks." Ruby threw open a washer lid, tossing items in at a fast pace. "You're dressed too, I see. Were you cold?"

"Uh-huh. It might rain this afternoon, they say." Doreen was pulling clothes from a dryer. Curiosity ate at Doreen. "When did you get back from Indiana? And where are you living now?"

"I came back a few days ago, and I'm in a place in Riverside. Let me write down my address and phone for you."

"Thanks. You're getting to be a regular here at Olive Canyon. You must like it."

Ruby paused in her washer loading. "Sure do. But sometimes I can't help overhearing things, you know, like sometimes when Dominic hollers. I feel so bad for you, taking all that guff from him." She rubbed one hand against the other.

Doreen, folding a T-shirt, looked up at her friend. She was touched by the concern. "He only drinks in the evenings. He really doesn't mean anything by all that noise. He gets a few Manhattans in him and doesn't know what he's saying, so I just mostly ignore his yelling. I just keep quiet. If I say anything at all he just yells louder."

"I don't like to butt into somebody else's business, but if you ever need a body to talk to, I'm here. Call me up any time."

"Thanks, Ruby. You're a real friend." Picking up her laundry basket, she headed for the door. "See ya later." As Doreen walked toward the mobile home, her mind filled with last night's dream. She realized the same nightmare had haunted her off and on for months. In it she was struggling hard to run, straining as hard as she could, but her feet were stuck in black tar. She'd get one foot up a bit, but the other was stuck fast. She fought with all her strength to run away, but couldn't gain an inch. She was filled with panic, knew she had to get away — impossible! This scene repeated in her consciousness now, telling her something, but what? *What does it mean? It means I need to get away from something, or someone.*

That evening under an overcast sky, Dom and Doreen Pierce were soaking away their concerns in the Jacuzzi's bubbling, gurgling cauldron. It was late. They were alone, the other couples having removed themselves to go home, or to their campers. The air about their heads was chilly. The timer lights had gone off, allowing darkness to close in around them. The steamy water brought lassitude.

Dom said, "A detective from the police, Felix Trappe,

called today to set up an appointment for tomorrow to talk with us."

"I wonder if that means he thinks something is suspicious about Ronnie's death, and will talk with everyone who was at that party." Doreen pushed a squiggle of damp hair away from her face. "Maybe we can help him in some way. Did he mention the coroner's report?"

"He said she had water in her lungs and a fairly low blood-alcohol level, only .03."

"Poor Ronnie. I miss her so much—everyone will."

In spite of feeling guilty for disobeying Dom's orders, Doreen thought about the guilt or innocence of the other party goers. Ed and Mona Lott had been members of Olive Canyon for several years, but hadn't socialized with Doreen and Dom, other than to say, "Hello. How are you," until quite recently. After Mona lost the election to Veronica Corrigan several months ago, she had seemed bitterer than would be expected in a simple rivalry. Apparently that seat on the Olive Canyon Board of Directors meant more to Mona than it did to Veronica, but Ronnie's pleasant personality had won her the victory. Was Mona jealous enough to kill?

Ed and Mona Lott, both in their late thirties, liked to impress the world with their financial success by dressing expensively, driving new cars, and living high. Mona wasn't pretty or cute, but nevertheless was attractive, being tall and slim with hairdresser-maintained grooming. Mona had what seemed to Doreen a brittle quality, like a dried-out stick that would easily snap in two, unable to bend under stress. She took pleasure in one-upmanship, was a master at it. Ed Lott liked that, as long as he wasn't her victim.

All the old-timers at Olive Canyon knew of Mona's darker side—depressions that put her into treatment centers every few years. Mona and Doreen had become chummier lately, with Mona phoning at least once a week to chat. Even so, Doreen had not known the Lotts were swingers until she saw them at the swing party. Actually, until very recently, Doreen had been completely ignorant of the swing scene and its players, unaware that such activities even happened. *Ed was in the Group Room when I was there, so he didn't kill Veronica, but where was Mona at that time?*

Stretching out in the hot bubbly water, Doreen asked Dom, "Weren't you surprised that Sarah and Angelo Lamb were at the swing party? In all the time I've known them at Olive Canyon, I didn't know they were swingers. You never can tell about people. Those two don't fit my idea of swingers, especially Sarah with her round freckly face. She looks so darned innocent. She's told me about her flower beds, her gardening, the pet rabbits Angelo raises. I was impressed with their stories of how loving, considerate, handsome, intelligent, and talented—in other words, perfect—their only child Percy is, and how proud Angelo is to have his son working with him at the same factory."

Dom said, "I didn't know they were swingers, so I was a bit surprised too. I'm pretty sure I heard Percy died last year."

"What a blow that must have been to them. But, now that you mention it, they didn't come to Olive Canyon for quite a while. Guess that's why. Sarah never mentions Percy anymore."

Doreen told Dom about the time two years ago when she had gone into the snack bar at Olive Canyon for a cup of coffee, and upon leaving, had paused at the umbrella-table where the Lambs were eating.

Sarah Lamb said, "Come sit with us awhile," and poked the last of a sandwich into her mouth. She wore nothing but sunglasses and sandals. In her mid-forties, Sarah's dark-blonde locks were braided, and pinned up into a bun on top of her head. Her round face, pale and freckly, and gray-green eyes somehow gave Doreen the impression of drabness. Her skin, although liberally coated against sunburn, was too bright pink on the high points: nose, shoulders, breasts, belly, and thighs. *She would be wise to stay in the shade this afternoon,* Doreen thought.

"Thanks." After setting down her towel, Doreen plunked herself onto a white wrought-iron chair. "Perfect weather for sunbathing, isn't it. Sunny, warm, just enough breeze to keep it from feeling too hot." She peeled the paper away from one end of the chocolate bar she had removed from her satchel, the smell of the candy making her salivate.

Sun shining through the huge red umbrella centered above the table imparted a reddish hot glow to all beneath it.

Sarah said breathlessly, "Guess what. Our son Percy's been hired to work at the plant where Angelo works. Percy's been trying to get a job there for months, and he finally made it! He's so excited. And Angelo too." She looked at her husband, nodding, as if to help him agree with her.

Angelo said, "The kid'll make us proud. He's a good

worker, a good boy." He swirled each morsel of French fry in his ketchup before popping it into his mouth. He had a handsome face with shiny dark eyes, a straight strong nose, a full sensuous mouth, and a mop of black wavy hair. His was a square face above a square sturdy frame, prominent muscles rippling as he moved, and cascades of black curly hair pouring down his body, front and back, overflowing onto his thighs, and trickling down his lower legs.

When Doreen got up to leave the table, Sarah and Angelo were still discussing Percy. Doreen concluded her description of the episode with, "And that's the way they are, really overboard about their boy Percy."

Dom said, "That's the way the conversation went when they chatted with me at the office one day awhile back." He got out of the hot water and grabbed a towel.

Doreen hauled herself out of the Jacuzzi. "Percy was so young—only in his early twenties—what caused his death?" she asked, wrapping up in her robe and sliding her feet into thong sandals.

"I don't know. Perhaps an illness. Maybe an auto accident?"

CHAPTER 13

In the morning Detective Felix Trappe arrived punctually at Dominic and Doreen Pierces' Olive Canyon mobile home. When Felix had requested an appointment, Dom had decided it would be more fun to have the detective meet them at Olive Canyon than their Long Beach home. Their inclination was to do the interview in the nude, and watch the man's expression when Doreen greeted him at the door of the mobile home. Only at the last moment did they put on clothing. As he entered, Doreen closed the door and invited him to sit down, omitting the standard "Make yourself comfortable" nudist offer, assuming that the cop would not have any idea what it meant.

Felix stuffed his rotundity into a beige-and-white-striped armchair, his eyes missing nothing. He looked very warm, somewhat red-faced, in a brown suit with jacket and tie. He refused a cold drink or hot coffee. Dominic and Doreen sat opposite him on the sofa. The room was cheery, with silk flowers and live plants, daylight flowing in the many windows.

Felix glanced at his notes. "You're the manager of this nudist col, uh, resort. Correct?"

Dominic said, "Correct," feeling like Felix's eyes were drilling through him. He thought, *I'm glad I've no reason to lie to this man. He could make you squirm just looking at you.*

"Was the victim a close friend, or just a casual

acquaintance?"

"We're cousins, were cousins, that is," Doreen said. "I loved her. We were closer than sisters."

Turning his gaze on Dominic, "How did you feel about Mrs. Corrigan?"

"I was very fond of her. We've been friends for many years, since Doreen and I got married."

Doreen said, "I don't believe she drowned accidentally."

Trappe's eyes widened in surprise. "Why not?" His ears seemed to come forward like a cat's.

"I saw Veronica swim many, many times. Because of her missing foot she had developed strong upper body muscles to compensate. And besides, she wasn't much of a drinker, preferred weak drinks, and never showed any effect from the alcohol. Have you talked with her husband Jake about that?" Doreen shifted a pillow as she spoke.

"Yes. He thinks it was an accident. What can you tell me about Jake Corrigan, how he treated Veronica, did they argue, did he hit her?"

Dom said, "I've never seen them fight or argue. Jake seems very self-centered, I'd say, but not abusive. I think they were relatively content as a couple."

Felix turned to Doreen, asking, "What do you think?"

"I agree." She thought, *Felix's face and shaggy pale hair remind me of a lion. I'll bet he hangs on like a lion to his prey, too.* She sat with her hands resting on her lap.

"Where did Ruby Falstaff fit in? What is it with her and Jake Corrigan?" Felix was sweating profusely, mopping his brow with a large white handkerchief.

Dom said, "I think they're just good friends. Ruby and

Elliott, her late husband, and Jake and Veronica Corrigan were friendly when the Falstaffs were here on vacation a while back. The four of them socialized and played a lot of tennis together. Nothing more, as far as I know."

Doreen added, "Veronica and Jake kept in touch with Ruby, after Ruby went back to Indiana to bury her husband Elliott, who died here from a heart attack. That's where his family lives."

Felix made notes, nodding his head. "About the swing party, did you know everyone there?"

Dom said, "We knew them all as Olive Canyon members. We'd met them here."

After a pause Doreen said, "Veronica was very friendly—people liked her." Doreen shifted in her seat, hesitated, then decided to say what was on her mind. "There's one person I can think of who wasn't happy with Veronica. Mona Lott lost an election to her, but it was only for a seat on the board of directors here, not a big deal to win or lose. Surely not enough to kill over."

Felix leaned forward, his attention fixed on Doreen. "You never can tell how important that may have been to Mrs. Lott. What else can you tell me about her?"

Doreen agonized for a few long seconds over whether or not she should mention Mona's depressions. She decided to keep quiet on that topic, for now anyway. "She's high-strung, a bit of a cold fish, aloof, usually, but I doubt she'd harm anyone. Doesn't seem the type."

In a voice reminiscent of a lion's growl, he asked questions about the others at the swing party, each person on his list. He scribbled down their replies. Standing at the door on his way out, he said, "Thanks for your help." As he climbed into his Volvo sedan, he characterized the Pierces as honest. They did not seem to him to be the kind of people he had expected swingers or nudists to be.

As soon as the detective's car was out of sight, Doreen and Dom improved their comfort level by shedding their clothing. It was a very warm day.

Doreen said, "I'll go see if the mail's in yet." A big mailbox by the entrance gate yielded some personal mail forwarded by a neighbor, and a stack of club-related material, which she left in the office with Howard Brill, the gatekeeper. Checking the return addresses as she entered the mobile, she said, "Here's one from IRS. It's about my business."

"What do they want?"

She ripped open the envelope, and unfolded the stiff white paper before speaking. "They're gonna do an audit of my business tax return. What a pain!"

"Don't worry about it. It'll be fine. I've been doing your taxes—I know they're right." His superior Mr. Perfect tone grated.

"You're right—no sweat. I'll just make an appointment as soon as possible, and get it over with. You'll go with me, won't you?"

Chapter 14

Later in the day, clouds had boiled over the tops of the mountains from the west, and were sprinkling on the resort. However, Chairperson Doreen had months ago scheduled a meeting of the Mr. and Ms. Nude World Annual Pageant Committee for 2 p.m., so she and Dom drove to the community room, parking close to it. When they entered, several others were already there, dressed appropriately for the wet, cool weather, sipping coffee and chatting. She helped herself to a mug of steaming coffee, found a seat at the green-topped ping-pong table, and dug out a chocolate bar from her voluminous pocketbook. Her Lincolnesque husband sat next to her with his coffee.

The room was brightly lit. Sunshine yellow paint covered the concrete-block interior. Several coin-operated candy and soda vending machines occupied one wall. At the far end from the ping-pong area, two pool tables with lamps hanging down over them squatted expectantly, racks of cue sticks nearby.

Mona Lott, pale and thin, sat across from the Pierces, smoking and fidgeting, manicured nails wine red. Six other members, the same ones as last year, arranged themselves around the big green table. The business discussion didn't last long. When it ended most of the participants left. Mona rushed over to speak to Dominic. She was so tall she was almost eye to eye with Dom, her short blonde hair perfect in spite of the weather. She gushed to him how shocked she had been when Veronica was found dead.

Then she said, "Too bad Veronica was such a drinker—she might be alive today. She always did a lot of boozing at the parties. She didn't seem to enjoy them very much. It made me wonder if she only went to them because Jake forced her to go or something. Not that it's any of my business how much liquor she drank, but…" Red faced, she muttered something as she turned, pushed open the door, and clutching her London Fog coat and her leather handbag, ran out into the soft drizzle.

Doreen watched Mona leave, thinking, *Damn, I'd hoped to pump her a bit about her relationship with Veronica.*

Veronica Corrigan's memorial service at the funeral home drew her many friends and relatives. On the previous day, Veronica's remains had been cremated, and the ashes scattered near the chapel on the high bluff at Olive Canyon. While people were milling about prior to settling down, Doreen circulated, speaking with everyone, making mental notes regarding what she considered suspicious actions, expressions, or body language. She thought, *Sorry, Dom, I just can't stop looking for Veronica's killer.*

Jake Corrigan seemed to be adjusting to the loss of his wife. Grieving, yes, most definitely, Doreen thought, but holding up pretty well. Ruby Falstaff stayed close to Jake, comforting him, perhaps because she too had recently lost a spouse. *Did they kill Veronica? Or just Ruby? Or just Jake? I doubt it. Jake sure does have motive though—all that insurance money.*

Chuck and Maggie Fast spoke with Jake and Ruby, then with everyone who had been at the infamous party. They had both been in the Group Room scene with Doreen, so they were in the clear.

Barbara Sweet, who had also been in the Group Room when Doreen was, appeared to be very sad, even somewhat nervous, squirming and restless. She told Doreen she had never attended "one of these affairs" before, and she wished her friend Dick Weiner or someone had been along for support, but Dick had an urgent business commitment. *Did he kill Veronica? Why would he?* Doreen invited Barbara to sit next to her, which she did. Barbara looked like an older heavier Barbie Doll, stiff and unreal, wearing too much make-up. Doreen wasn't well acquainted with Dick Weiner and Barbara Sweet, had no idea what connections Dick might have had with Veronica or Jake Corrigan. Did they have more than their nudist affiliation and swing parties in common. *What is Dick's urgent business today? Is he afraid to show up here because he killed Veronica?*

Ed and Mona Lott sat one row in front of the Pierces. Ed remained calm, hardly moving a hair. He was off the hook, anyway, another Group Room participant. Mona tapped first one foot then the other, inspected her long red fingernails, then started to chew on one, stopping abruptly when she realized what she was doing. She peered around as if looking for someone. Doreen figured part of Mona's problem was the No Smoking sign, as tobacco-addicted as Mona was. *Would she have come here today if she murdered Veronica? Who's missing? Maybe the killer wouldn't show anyway. Then again, if I had killed her, and wanted to look innocent, I'd be at this service for sure.*

Seeing that Angelo and Sarah Lamb were not present, she figured they could be forgiven, considering they were still mourning for Percy. They would be unable to face another depressing service such as this for a long time.

Ross and Cynthia Meissen did not attend, she noted, wondering why not. She failed to realize that one other party attendee was missing, Ruby's escort at the party, Avery Trent.

Heavy scent from flowers too much in abundance, and the dreary droning organ music added their particular gloom to the ambience for Doreen. Ever since her own baby's funeral, organ sounds revived the anguish as if it had just happened yesterday. Doreen silently heaved a sigh of relief when the ordeal ended.

Jake had invited Ruby and Doreen and Dominic to his house afterward. He wanted them to stay with him a while longer—he didn't want to be alone. The house had become a cold and empty shell. He fixed them all a drink.

"We were really surprised to see you at the swing party, Ruby," Doreen said, settling into a comfortable chair.

Jake said, "When Veronica phoned Ruby a few weeks ago, Ruby was getting ready to move back to California, so we expected to see her."

Ruby nodded agreement and smiled.

"That man at the party with you, I didn't recognize him." Doreen said.

"Avery Trent. He's just someone I'd picked up in a bar so I could be admitted to the party. Have to go there in couples, of course."

Jake puffed on a cigar, his mind elsewhere. His face lost its placid quality as he said, "Boy, this is a lonely place now. It's gonna be tough runnin' the business without Veronica. She was the one who ordered the food and drinks, kept the books ya know. She was the brains of our business."

"She was a special person. I miss her so much." Tears burned. Doreen blinked them away and asked, "Do you have someone else to cover Ronnie's truck route?" Jake's cigar's stench was cloying, but Doreen tolerated it without complaint.

"Yeah, a guy who helped us out a few times when we went on vacations. He's been lookin' to work full time. He'll be glad to get the job."

"That's good. Ronnie's regular customers will really miss her, I'm sure."

To change the subject, Dominic said, "We heard you bought a brand new catering truck. How do you like it?"

"It's a beauty. The old one was about to drop in its tracks. This one should last a lotta years—it cost plenty." Jake put down his stogy, got up and headed toward the garage. "Come on. I'll show it to you."

The three of them poked around the new vehicle, Jake proudly explaining its marvels. "Maybe I'll replace the other old truck with one just like this. After I come back from my trip."

Doreen's eyebrows slid up an inch. "Where are you going? And when?"

"Europe, London, Ireland, places we—Veronica and

me—never went, and always wanted to." Jake seemed close to tears. Then his face brightened. "I may not go alone. Ruby's been everywhere. I've almost convinced her to come along as my guide. Haven't decided when though."

Dom said, "That's great. A change of scenery will do you good."

Doreen thought, *Yup, murderers need a change of scenery too. Hmmph.*

CHAPTER 15

At home in Long Beach, Doreen, revising a dress design for the umpteenth time, was getting frustrated. It was 7 p.m. and she had put in a long and busy day. *I need a break—been at this long enough. Where's my chocolate? Guess I'll have some tea, too.* She leaned back in her desk chair, tossing her feet up on the desk. A nagging subconscious thought emerged from deep in her mind. *What if Dom killed Veronica? Maybe that's why he insisted that it was an accident. Why would he do that? Was he jealous of our close relationship? He's never been really close to anyone, even me. Nah, he's not a killer. Or is he? I'll just snoop around his desk for anything to connect him to the time bomb or the murder. I hope nothing turns up.*

She finished her snack, threw the candy wrapper in the trash. In the kitchen she rinsed her cup and put it on the counter. She checked around the house to be sure she was alone. Dom was out, she didn't know where, but his car was gone. Her Honda Accord sat solo in the garage.

Her muscles knotted in trepidation; guilt hounded her for even suspecting her husband. Theirs had always been a trusting relationship, and betrayal of that trust made her stomach churn. She crept into their bedroom. Carefully she pulled out each dresser drawer, replacing each moved item to its previous location. Nothing amiss there. She took a deep breath, and continued. Investigating the pockets of the clothing hanging in his closet rewarded her with zip. She paused to listen.

At his desk she started by looking at receipts—nothing out of line there. Next the file drawer, nothing exciting. She opened his checkbook. Before she read a word a creepy feeling came over her, as if she were being watched. She hadn't heard the car or the door, but she glanced up anyway. Standing in the doorway with his arms folded, Dom glared at her. "What's this all about?" he growled. His gray-green eyes were ferocious slits in a bunched-up face.

"Uh, well, I… "

"Never mind. I don't care. I just don't care anymore about you, about us."

He's had a few Manhattans already—he's nasty. "I was going to get supper ready, but then I wondered if you had paid the power bill yet. I don't know why that question suddenly came to mind, but it did. So here I am."

"You know I hate nosy people, especially nosy women." He turned and stomped down the hall.

Doreen clamped her mouth shut, dropped the checkbook, scooted past him and went straight to the kitchen. She had lately begun to realize just how much Dominic disliked women, all women, and wondered if he would ever change. She thought not. When Dominic's mother was alive, Doreen had recognized what she thought of as a love/hate relationship between her and her son. *The honeymoon's over for us, has been for a long, long time.*

That evening she convinced herself that Dominic, her husband of many years, had killed her cousin for two reasons: first, because he hates women in general, and

88

second, because he was jealous of the close bond between Dory and her cousin—a bond that Dom had never experienced, would never be capable of. But what a dilemma that caused. She couldn't tell anyone—he'd kill her if he found out. She had no proof. What if he suspected she knew? Would he kill her too? Not if she continued to act just exactly the same, never letting him think for a second she considered him the killer. She felt fairly safe as long as she followed that plan. That night she slept poorly, in short naps, watching her husband snooze comfortably, determined to be wary of even the slightest change she might notice in his behavior. Around three in the morning she finally dozed off, only to awaken at six.

Chapter 16

Several days later, they were again home in Long Beach, seated in the dining room at the round oak table with its yellow, gold, and green silk-flower centerpiece on a lace doily, looking through the pile of mail that had accumulated. The place was homey with warm oak furniture, a braided rug, framed prints, houseplants, and an oak-framed mirror. White ruffled curtains decorated the open windows. Doreen loved decorating. Outside, a miniature jungle encroached aggressively as if to take over the entire quarter acre of land—split-leaf philodendron and elephant ears taller than the house, plum, avocado, lemon, lime, and peach trees, bird-of-paradise, red-blooming hibiscus, bougainvillea, honeysuckle, and several other vines. Sparrows, robins, and hummingbirds chirped, twittered, and fluttered.

Doreen said, "Jake acts like he's already spending the insurance settlement, two new catering trucks and some overseas travel. With Ruby perhaps."

"Yeah. So what? It's not your business."

Dom went to the window and stared at the robins poking around in the grass.

Doreen was sorting the mail, one pile for reading, the other for throw-away.

"Here's another letter from IRS. Now what? When I phoned for an appointment the person told me they were still working on my case, and would let me know.

Imagine, my case! Like I'm a criminal." Doreen spread the papers out and began reading. "It says I have ten days to provide them with evidence of most of my business deductions. All those receipts are in the files at the studio. Guess I'll have to dig out the ones they want to see. Tomorrow." Since Dominic didn't respond, in fact, ignored her, she said no more. She wasn't concerned since she thought she knew right where everything she needed could be found. Just a lot of unnecessary bother.

After making out her list for a grocery-shopping trip, Doreen found Dominic tinkering with a loose hinge on the back screen door. She told him she was going shopping, and left.

Parking in the little strip mall lot near the Market Basket, she stepped out of the Honda and spotted Ruby two cars away, having just emerged from her red top-down convertible.

"Ruby Falstaff. What a surprise. How are you?" Doreen hurried in Ruby's direction.

Ruby seemed genuinely pleased. "How good to see you. I was just about to do some shopping. You too?" They hugged one another.

"Me too. How about a cuppa coffee first?"

"Okay. Sounds good. This coffee shop?" Ruby nodded toward the New Age Coffee Shop that was two doors away from the Market Basket.

While stirring sugar and cream into her coffee, Doreen said, "How've you been?" as she envied Ruby's trim shape in a pale green shirtwaist dress. She almost fished out a chocolate bar, but due to Ruby's influence, she overcame the urge.

"Pretty good. You?" The booth they occupied sported

worn Naugahyde and scarred Formica, but the place was clean and bright.

"Okay." Doreen sighed. "Terribly upset about Veronica." Tears welled up and stung her eyes. "She was so terrific." She brushed a tear away and dug into her big handbag for a tissue.

"It's been hard on all of us," Ruby said, sipping at her black coffee. "She was so sweet, a really cheerful and wonderful person."

Doreen wiped at her eyes and nose with a Kleenex. "And worse for you, with your husband gone so recently." Doreen said as Ruby nodded in agreement, "So, are you back in California to stay?"

"Yep. I've adopted the State of California for my own." Her face lit up. "I feel like I've come home."

"Good. I'm glad to hear it. Does that mean we'll be seeing more of you at Olive Canyon?"

Laughing, Ruby said, "You crack me up. Seeing more of me at Olive Canyon, a nudist resort. That's a good one. You'll see *all* of me, in the flesh."

With a grin and a raised hand Doreen said, "Okay, okay."

"I'll probably show up there with Jake Corrigan now and then. We're kind of a support group for each other these days, you know. He seems awfully macho at times, but he really loved Veronica a lot. It was a dreadful accident."

Doreen thought, *"Accident." She doesn't seem to think it was murder.* "We'll all look forward to having both of you show up at camp. Have you heard from Jake recently? Are you going to travel with him?"

"I phoned yesterday to see how he was doing. He's

realized he can't go anywhere much because he has to run the business. When he retires, maybe." Ruby put her elbows on the table and clasped her hands. "He's suffering, I can tell, but he always plays macho man."

Doreen leaned across the table toward Ruby, held both of Ruby's hands, and listed the reasons she believed her cousin's death was murder, not accidental. Ruby soaked up the information, agreeing. Doreen sat back.

"She couldn't have had enemies! Why would anyone kill Veronica?" Ruby asked.

"I need to know that as much as you do. I was trying to gather information, clues really, but Dominic has forbidden me to do any more. That's why he left—I wouldn't leave the subject alone after he'd ordered me to. That, and he'd had too much to drink." Powerlessness made Doreen sag all over. She almost whispered, "I want to help. But he's right, it's too dangerous."

Ruby the rebel spoke up in sharp tones. "I've always done what I wanted, right or wrong. It's hard for me to watch you let your husband dominate you that way, and not say anything. You may put yourself in danger, but I say, if that's what you want to do, and that's what you need to do for your own peace of mind, then do it!"

Doreen sat up straight as if jerked upward by the top of her head. "You're right, absolutely right. I'll continue asking questions. I'll do it for Ronnie. If Dom doesn't approve, too bad." She smacked the table. A smile crinkled around her eyes, and joy lit her face like a spotlight. For the first time since her cousin's death, she felt alive, energized.

"Atta girl! Way to go!"

Then Doreen turned her head away, withdrawing.

"What's the matter? Are you okay?"

Wiping at tears on her cheeks, she said, "This could mean the end of my marriage. I still love him. I've never stood up to Dom before. I don't know what'll happen, how he'll take it. I don't know if I can do it."

"I spoke outta turn. Don't listen to me."

"I think you're right about him dominating me. I just never thought of it that way before. But I'm not sure if I can handle the consequences. I'll have to give this whole thing a lot of thought before I do anything." She gulped some coffee.

To change the topic, Ruby asked, "Have you and Dom been swingers very long?"

Doreen set down her empty coffee mug. "No. Actually, that was our first. What an introduction to swinging!"

"Too bad you picked that particular night for your first. But, hey, there's gotta be a first time. Elliott and I were swingers for years."

The young man who came and refilled their mugs had a smirk on his face—listening to this conversation was really fun. Too bad he had to go back to the kitchen.

Doreen opened her mouth, then hesitated. "I have an awfully personal question. Don't answer it if you don't want to."

"Go ahead, ask. I have nothing to hide."

"How many men do you usually go with at a party?" Doreen blushed as she asked.

"Generally, two. Jake's one, of course." With an impish twinkle she added, "You must have noticed how he's built—like a stud horse. Wouldn't want to pass that up." She took a sip from her mug. "And then someone else. Dick Weiner was the other one that night. To think, I was just having fun, playing around, while my friend Veronica was drowning." She quickly wiped at a trickle of tears with the back of her hand. "Maybe I could have saved her. If only I'd known."

So Ruby's probably off the hook, and Dick, as well. "I feel that way too. Ronnie was my best friend as well as my cousin. We were closer than sisters."

Soon the women left to do the errands they'd come to do.

When Doreen arrived home with the groceries, she related some of the conversation to Dom, adding that she now felt quite certain Ruby was innocent of Veronica's death.

Dom growled, "Keep your nosy self out of it, Doreen! That's an order."

She meekly stored away the foods, saying nothing more. *I shouldn't have told him about meeting Ruby. Why am I always doing or saying something wrong? I just don't seem to able to stand up to him like I should. I'm too afraid he'll fly into a tantrum.*

The old familiar nightmare tormented her sleep, as it so often did, with Doreen desperate to run away from something. The tar under her feet prevented her escape.

CHAPTER 17

The following morning promised a cooler day, a sprinkle of nighttime showers having cleared the air. Doreen arose thinking about the conversation she had had with Elmore May the previous evening. She pinned up her hair, glanced at the time, 7:45, donned a shower cap, and started her wake-up shower. Since Elmore was manager of the swing parties, she had phoned him to ask if he could think of anything different about the party at which Veronica died.

"Was there anything out of the ordinary about the crowd that attended? Something said or done that was unusual?"

"The lady police detective, what's her name, Jackson, and Detective Trappe asked me that too," he said, "and as I told them it was a very run-of-the-mill evening until...you know."

"Were there other first-timers like Dominic and me? Or was it mostly the same folks attending every week?"

"You and your husband were the only first-timers that evening. I usually see the same faces week after week. But wait a minute—I just remembered. That was the first time I'd seen the Lambs in a long time. They used to be regulars, seldom missed a week, and then they just stopped showing up. I never knew why. Thought maybe they'd moved away or something. It was good to have them back—nice folks."

"Was anything changed about them?"

"Not that I noticed. They did leave early though."

"Was that their usual routine?"

"No. Most everyone stays at least until 11:30, and some never leave before 2 a.m. The Lambs usually left around midnight. But that night Mrs. Lamb became ill, so they went home at 10."

Doreen was satisfied that Mr. May had given her all the helpful information he could. It was inconceivable to imagine Sarah or Angelo killing Veronica—what motive would they possibly have? They couldn't be killers; they loved their child, their pets and plants. People who had so much love just couldn't kill. However, she mentally filed their names away in her "suspect" file. *Almost everyone at the party had the opportunity and the means, but who had a reason to want Ronnie dead?* Whenever she though about motive, only Jake or Ruby, or both, looked guilty. But how to prove it? Jake didn't seem like a murderer, and she couldn't believe that about Ruby. She was pretty sure Dominic was innocent. She shut off the water and reached for her bath towel. The little bathroom clock read 8 a.m.

Dom was right about the danger, but why did he even talk about danger if he truly thought it had been an accident? Doreen felt that nothing could happen to her. Besides, she was being extra careful to make her conversations sound casual and friendly, not snoopy, so who would figure out why she was asking questions? Having copied down all the swingers' phone numbers from the records in the office at Olive Canyon, she unwrapped a chocolate bar, took a bite and a deep breath, and dialed the Lambs, hoping to hear Sarah at the other end. It was Angelo who answered, but she was prepared, or so she thought.

After a brief greeting, and without pausing for breath, Doreen spit out words like bullets from a firing squad. "I heard you and Sarah were at the swing party the other night, and wouldn't you know, I didn't see either one of you there. It was our first time, and I guess I just missed you in all the excitement of Veronica's murder. I didn't know you were swingers until I heard Mr. May say you'd been there, but that you'd left early. Anyway, that's neither here nor there. What I called about was to ask Sarah if she can replace a woman on the Nude World Pageant Committee, one who's moving to Texas next week."

"Who said she was murdered? It was an accident— that's what the papers said." He snarled, "She was a boozer. Besides, I don't see it's any of your business," thinking fast he added, "if we go to the parties or not."

I shouldn't have said that. Better try to calm him down. "You're right. It isn't my business. Is Sarah home? I'd like to speak with her, please."

"Sarah's not home just now. Probably be back by 2 or 3 o'clock. I doubt she'd be willing to get involved in the pageant thing though. She hasn't been herself since our son died."

"I'm sorry to hear that. I mean, I'm not sorry she wouldn't want to get involved with the pageant. That's no big deal, but I'm sorry your son died—I lost a daughter so I know how awful it must be for you." Doreen sucked in some air and continued. "You know, I just recently heard about Percy, and I'm awfully sad about that. You two were so proud of him—he must have been a wonderful son." She thought, *I'm babbling on and on like a fool. I wish Sarah had answered the phone.*

"He was the best! Had a great future ahead of him. He was gonna start night classes at the junior college." Angelo's voice suddenly became angry. "That's all over now. I don't want to talk about it," he barked.

Doreen started to ask Angelo to tell Sarah that she'd called when Angelo hung up on her in mid-sentence.

Later Doreen tried again—this time all ready to just hang up if Angelo answered—and got through to Sarah. They had never been close friends, merely acquaintances who had their nudist affiliation in common.

"Sarah, I wondered if you would like to help us with the Nude World Pageant at Olive Canyon this year. We, the committee I mean, thought perhaps you'd be willing to fill in for Mary Ellen since she's moving to Texas next week."

"I'd love to. It's time for me to get out and do things again, get involved with other people," Sarah said, so softly that she was almost whispering.

"That's wonderful. It's a fun event. I'm sure you'll enjoy it." Doreen then asked, "Do you have a sore throat? I can hardly hear you."

"No. Angie's in the garden—I don't want him to hear me," she whispered. "I'm not sure Angie will let me do anything. But I can't stay here all the rest of my life. I'll talk with him about the pageant. I want to do it."

"That'll be terrific." Trying to gradually introduce the real reason for her call, Veronica's murder, Doreen said, "I heard about your loss only recently, Sarah, and I'm so sorry. Was Percy ill?"

"No. Didn't they tell you? It was suicide, last year. He

was depressed."

Shocked by the word, Doreen said, "Suicide...I'm sorry to hear that. I didn't know." Realizing this was not a good time to talk about her cousin's death, she asked "How are you doing?"

"I'm just taking life a day at a time."

No wonder Angelo was so upset. How awful for both of them.

When the phone rang in the late afternoon, Doreen answered it. Sarah Lamb's high-pitched voice was very clear on the other end.

"Doreen! We need to talk. I'm worried. I don't know who else to turn to."

"Sure. When do you want to—" *Click.* Dial tone. Doreen dialed Sarah's number, but no one answered. *I wonder what that was all about. I'll try again in the morning.*

By 9 that evening, Dom had said only a few words to Doreen. She had prepared one of his favorite dinners— noodles and sausage—but he had been drinking Manhattans for hours. He scowled in silence while he ate the meal. She hated it when he was like this, keeping her on edge for fear he'd yell at her. Instead he spoke quietly, in a cold tone that chilled her. "I'm leaving. I don't want to hear from you or see you. Maybe I'll be back and maybe I won't." With that, he rose from the table, packed a few things and drove away.

Doreen was devastated. She cried a while, then wiped her eyes and phoned Ruby, pouring out her sad tale. Ruby offered to come and stay with Doreen, or for Doreen to go there, as long as needed.

"Thanks. You're a real friend, Ruby. I just had to tell

someone my sad tale, but honestly, I feel better now.
Being able to talk about it helps a lot."

"You sure you're all right?"

"Come to think of it, maybe I'll even enjoy not having
him here. For a little while. I can watch the TV shows I like,
instead of his choices. I have a novel to read, too. He
always insists I watch TV with him, even when I'd rather
read." She paused briefly, thinking about how she might
pry information out of Ruby, to see if Jake Corrigan gave
any clues that he had killed his wife. Nothing sensible
came to mind. Soon they said their goodbyes and hung up.

Doreen, alone for the night, cuddled into her favorite
recliner chair to read. After several pages she realized she
didn't have any idea what she'd read—her mind was
involved with her cousin's death and Dom's departure.
Slumped into the enfolding warmth of the chair, she felt
depressed, unloved, rejected, unwanted, and so alone.
Her father had been a cold and distant authority figure,
was that way until he died. Her mother had succumbed
to pneumonia many years ago, and Doreen still missed
her, and figured she always would. She never had
siblings. Now Ronnie was gone, and Dom. Was she such
an awful person? Why was life treating her this way?

She sighed and shut off the reading lamp, leaving only
a tiny glow from a hallway nightlight. The sliding glass
doors looked out onto the back of the house where the
jungle-like garden and trees were. The dense darkness
out there was thick and heavy with just the merest hint of
light filtering through from a distant street light. She
allowed her vision to focus on nothing, letting her
thoughts drift. Always the same questions: the killer,
who and why?

Startled out of her meditation by the telephone, she collected her wits and said, "Hello." None of her friends ever called this late in the evening, 10:30. She stiffened in anticipation.

"You're next." *Click.* A muffled gravelly deep voice, then a dial tone. She wasn't sure she'd heard it right. *Maybe he said something else. Must have been. Why me?*

She jumped up, her heart in her mouth, locking each door and window, and closing drapes, pulling shades down. She moved around in the gloom, knowing she couldn't be seen from outside so readily if it was dark inside the house. A man's voice, for sure! Fear grabbed her by the throat—her mouth went dry. She felt shaky, weak. She sat down. *Now I wish Dom was home. Or maybe that was Dom that called. No, he wouldn't. I'll just phone the mobile home and tell him what happened. Maybe he'll come home.*

Dom's number rang and rang, then the answering machine picked up and she listened to the outgoing announcement. She left a brief message telling him of the strange call. Gradually the fear receded as she played the voice over and over in her mind, convincing herself she didn't know what the words were, and maybe it was just a wrong number. Before she retired for the night, though, she rechecked the doors and windows. She had begun to relax now, having convinced herself that she was mistaken, and what she thought she heard was not really what was said. Deciding it was probably nothing, she did not tell the police.

Checking a front window, she peeked out. Across the street on the neighbor's lawn, almost hidden by a large hibiscus bush, she saw the moving glow of the lit end of a cigarette. *It must be Dom—he smokes. He's the killer! Now he's after me!* She broke out in sweat. She picked up the phone to call 9-1-1. Her tongue glued itself to the roof of her mouth. Then she remembered, their neighbor Arnold Worthington often smoked out there when he couldn't sleep. She went to the kitchen, poured out a few ounces of wine, added ice and a like amount of cold water, and sat down to drink it. *There, now. This'll help me get to sleep. What a night so far! I've got myself in a tizzy over nothing.*

Chapter 18

In the morning she dialed Sarah's home number, but no one answered. Phoning Ruby, Doreen said in a strong voice, "Guess what. I've decided. Even if it means divorce, I'm going to do what I think is right."

"Wow! You've got backbone, Doreen. Hope everything works out for you."

"It'll work out, one way or the other. No more being ordered around for me."

Doreen told her friend about the frightening events of yesterday, adding that she was mistaken about the scary phone call, just as she was about the neighbor across the street's smoking on his front lawn. They chatted a while longer. Doreen put the phone down feeling like she could take on the world.

She dressed and drove her gray Honda to her business, Larger Women's Fashions. When she entered her studio, the manager rushed to her saying, "I'm so glad you're here. I was just about to call you. Bad news. Roberto had a big tiff with his roomie. He won't be coming in for a while."

Roberto Giordano was a talented designer whom Doreen had hired a few years ago. He was artistic, temperamental, and gay. He had insisted on taking the responsibility for the upcoming benefit fashion show, a motion Doreen had gladly seconded.

"What do you mean?"

"His roomie Phonso says he's gone to Hawaii. Doesn't know when he'll be back."

"Great! And meanwhile he promised me he'd do that fashion show that's coming up soon. What's he thinking of?" Grumbling and mumbling to herself, Doreen gathered the items for the IRS audit into a large cardboard carton, intending to sort through everything in the box and have it all ready and in order for her appointment. She lugged the box to her car, hoisting it into the trunk. She would have to prepare for the fashion show without Roberto's assistance, and that meant putting in a lot more hours of work at the studio. It was too close to the scheduled date—too many gears were already moving—to postpone the show. Her brow furrowed as she reviewed the essentials. She sat in the car making notes of things to do, people to call, details too urgent to be neglected. *Roberto, IRS, time bombs, Ronnie, Dom—what next?* She sighed.

That afternoon found Doreen and Mona Lott in a hospital room talking quietly to one another. The patient, Sarah Lamb, was napping. She was very pale but otherwise appeared okay—no IV or monitoring. Mona had phoned to tell Doreen that Sarah had been admitted as a patient after having severe head pain and fainting. They agreed to drive together in Doreen's car to the medical center in Los Angeles to visit.

Mona said, "I've been wanting to get together with you anyway, Doreen." She hesitated. "There's something I'd like to discuss, ah, a sort of a confession really."

"What's it about?" Doreen's mind jumped to the weird phone call.

"You remember the board elections at OC?"

The door swung inward, propelled by a husky LVN with a stethoscope hanging around her neck, followed by a green-garbed male attendant with a gurney.

"Sorry, folks. We're taking her to X-ray." Sarah's eyes popped open.

Mona went to the bedside and patted Sarah's arm, saying, "We'll be back. You concentrate on getting better, you hear?"

Sarah groped under her pillow, her hand coming out with a tissue. She surreptitiously slipped a folded paper into Doreen's hand, whispering, "Glad you came to see me, Doreen, and you too, Mona. Thanks."

As soon as she could manage it without being noticed, Doreen palmed the note, sliding it into a side pocket of her voluminous purse. She and Mona edged around the stretcher and left. With all the other pressing problems, the note remained in Doreen's purse, forgotten.

CHAPTER 19

The following weekend's hot weather brought a large crowd, including Doreen, to Olive Canyon. She noticed Dom playing on a volleyball team, but they still hadn't spoken. She was living in Long Beach, he at Olive Canyon.

As usual, Doreen socialized with one group after another, chatting with many people, making a special effort to mingle with the swingers who had attended the party the night her cousin Ronnie had been killed.

Doreen knew that Chuck and Maggie Fast were owners of a health club, and practiced what they preached. That is, except for deliberately exposing their hides to the sun. They exercised, hiked, biked, you name it, they did it. They were vegetarians too. And now Doreen knew that they were swingers as well. Both of them were in the Group Room at the time Doreen was, so she tucked them into her mental "not-a-suspect" folder. After a brief chat with them, she moved on.

Ed and Mona Lott were sunning on side-by-side blankets on the lawn when Doreen plopped down on her towel next to them. Mona was propped up on an elbow, reading. Ed was prone, sunning his gorgeous browned derriere, his head on his forearm turned to face his wife.

After ritual greetings, Ed asked Doreen, "Have you heard how Jake's holding up since Veronica's accident?"

"He's okay. It was a terrible shock, but he's managing."

"That's good." Then Ed lifted his head to say, "Veronica was such fun—she sure could tell jokes. We miss her."

Mona echoed, "Yeah. We miss her." Doreen didn't miss the flat tone of Mona's words. No enthusiasm, no real feeling, just the polite words required in polite society.

Mona rose to her feet after turning her paperback over to hold it open to the page where she had quit reading. Leaning close to Doreen who was seated on her towel, Mona whispered something to her. Doreen looked at her and nodded.

Mona said to Ed, "We'll be back soon." He waved. The two women strolled away toward the narrow dirt path leading to the chapel.

After they were out of sight, Doreen, eager to learn what it was that Mona didn't want the others to know, asked, "What's this all about?"

Mona didn't answer right away, but continued climbing up the hard-packed track with Doreen struggling to follow the younger woman's long-legged stride, under gnarled olive trees, around boulders, over thick roots until Mona was certain no one else could hear. She stopped, turning back to face Doreen.

"Do you think the police are looking into Veronica's death?" Her face was tense, creases marred the matte-finished flesh between her carefully-drawn eyebrows. Her short hair was salon-perfect, as always.

"Why do you ask that? And why ask *me*?" Doreen's skin was red, flushed from the effort of uphill trudging in the heat. To her right was a steep drop down into the canyon.

"I thought you might know more of what's going on, since you're the manager's wife." Mona was ineffectively fanning herself with her hands.

Doreen thought, *She's worried about something. Ed Lott was in the Group Room with me and the others when Veronica died, but where was Mona?* Doreen wiped at her sweaty face and wished she had a chocolate bar to munch while they rested, glad for the respite from the hill climbing. She declined to speak, to allow Mona more time to reveal what was on her mind.

Mona glanced around, making sure they were alone. "You know, I was awfully upset when I lost the election to Veronica. Of course, I got over it, but still..." She shrugged, still seeming to want to say more, to unburden herself.

"Go on." Doreen tried to study Mona's eyes to read what lay there, but sunglasses blocked their expression. *Did she get me way up here to kill me? She'll have to do it with her bare hands—she's nude, and has no place to carry a weapon.* Doreen shuffled a few steps away from the edge of the cliff, to the shelter of a tree, hoping her movements looked like she was merely seeking shade. Mona stayed where she was, her face tight, nervously rubbing her fingers against each other.

Holding her hands out in front of her, palms up, Doreen smiled and said quietly, "Mona, I get the impression something's on your mind. You can tell me, if it'll make you feel better. Whatever it is, it'll probably come out in the investigation anyway. Meanwhile, if you don't want me to, I won't tell a soul, not even Dominic."

Mona's tension dropped away, replaced by a little grin. She sighed. "Thanks. I appreciate your help in this.

I need to tell someone, but I'm afraid Ed won't believe me. It's been bothering me ever since I did it. It keeps growing bigger and bigger in my mind until sometimes I think I'll explode. Do you know how that is?"

Doreen's apprehension had multiplied as Mona spoke. *What if she killed Veronica? She shouldn't tell me. What's she planning to do once she tells me? Oh boy, that's a long drop to the bottom of the ravine!* Keeping her face, voice, and body as casual as possible, she said, "Sure. Everyone knows how that is."

Mona opened her mouth to say something, but instead, turned and ran like a gazelle farther up the path.

CHAPTER 20

Doreen thought, *Enough! I'm out of breath and overheated. She can spit it out some other time.*

She turned in disgust, heading back down the long hill for a cool drink at the snack bar. She ordered a coffee over ice, added sugar and cream, and put the charge on her tab, taking her frosty glass to an inside table where the overhead fans kept the air moving. Lunch could wait. Just as she drank the last mouthful, she spied Katie Brill outside. Dropping her paper cup in the trash, she hurried out to catch up with her friend.

"Katie. Good to see you." They hugged, then continued down the hill together.

"How have you been? I heard from Howie about you and the mister splittin' up." The path was dry and dusty, rutted in places. Doreen was getting hungry by now. Taking a chocolate bar from her canvas bag, she offered her companion some. The offer accepted, they both munched.

"I'm fine, thanks. We just need a little time. I expect we'll get back together soon."

"Humph. Maybe. I had a husband like your Dominic a long time ago. He thought he was the only one who could think, decide things. He was the big boss, worse than Dominic."

"Dom's not so bad." Doreen's heart had leaped, seeing him on the volleyball court. She loved him, no matter what.

"Like I was sayin', I've seen worse." Kate was waiting for Doreen to ask.

"What happened?"

"I left him. He wanted me back, but I had enough."

Doreen knew she'd be glad to have Dom come home, wished he would. "Were you really miserable when you were living with him?"

"We had some great times at first," Kate said. "I s'pose all couples do. But he was a drinker, like Dominic. He was real nice when he wasn't drinkin', but look out when he's drunk."

"I know what you mean. After you left him, did you miss him?"

"Sure. For a while. But I stopped getting stomach aches. After a time I knew I was much better off without him. No one needs that much upset."

"In that case, I guess it was good you divorced him. You and Howie seem to be pretty content. So it worked out for the best in the end."

"Howard is a dear sweet man. I'm lucky to have him." Then she added, "Your mister and that Angelo are gettin' to talk together a lot lately. Seems like they're drinkin' buddies some nights. Angelo's in your mobile home pretty often with Dominic."

"Really? I didn't know. Not that it matters. Angelo's a nice person. His wife Sarah's in the hospital, have you heard?"

"Nope. I never see her anymore. Hasn't been here in a coon's age. What happened to her?"

"I don't know. They're doing tests to find out what's wrong. I'll let you know as soon as I hear something."

Doreen felt perhaps Sarah's illness was due to her

son's death, and was probably a natural reaction. She could think of little else than her murdered cousin. "Katie, would you happen to know any reason why someone would want to get rid of my cousin Veronica?" She told her what she had told Ruby concerning her suspicion that Ronnie had been murdered. "Do you have any idea? Any clue?"

"Not yet, honey. I'll look in the tea leaves though, and let you in on anything that looks fishy. Glad to help. That Veronica was the prettiest, funniest, nicest one-legged lady I ever met."

They were approaching the rear of the gatekeeper's cabin. The pathway was shaded by the old olive trees, but here they came into a large clearing, a lawn, where the hot sun blazed. In the center were two shade trees, a brick barbecue, blackened from years of use, with picnic table and chairs nearby. To their right was the cabin, to their left the back of the mobile home. Both structures faced the main road. The cabin was of concrete block, painted pale yellow with brown trim. A screened room jutted out from the rear. Katie Brill had planted purple and white petunias and red geraniums to form a colorful border front and back. The mobile home was a simple white ten-wide with an added-on screened porch in the front. The gatehouse/office beyond was another pale yellow block structure, closer to the roadway and gate, but handy to both of the residences.

"We all loved her. I miss her a lot. And you, Doreen, you be careful. Watch behind your back. There may be a killer on the loose, and you're out there in the world all by yourself without the mister to protect you."

Katie turned and threw her arms around Doreen.

They hugged, and pecked each other's cheeks.

"Thanks for being my friend," Doreen said. "I'm heading home to Long Beach in a few minutes, but I'll give you a call soon."

"Be on your guard. I've seen danger in the tea leaves lately."

"I'll be careful." Aware that Katie often predicted events that came to pass, she shivered in apprehension.

At home in Long Beach, she made herself a BLT for lunch, then phoned Ruby to tell her about hiking up the hill after Mona. "You know, Mona's husband Ed was in sight when Veronica was drowned, but Mona could have been anywhere, even out in the pool with Veronica. Do you think she might have done it?"

"I guess that's possible. I wonder what she wanted to tell you up there on the hill." Ruby reached over to stir the beef stew she was making. She leaned closer and sniffed the steamy scent rising from the pot. *Good!*

After swallowing a mouthful of her BLT and washing it down with coffee, Doreen said, "She'll tell me sooner or later. She has to—she's about to burst." Then she told Ruby about Katie and her tea-leaf prediction of danger. Ruby pooh-poohed it as "utter foolishness," but Doreen remained convinced that Katie was right.

A little while later Dominic walked in the back door, looking cheerful. He set down his overnight bag and headed for Doreen. "Hello. I'm back."

Doreen went toward him saying, "Hi, stranger." She reached up. Putting their arms around each other, saying nothing, for a few minutes they both enjoyed the comfort of the others' presence. They acted as if nothing unusual had happened, and neither spoke of the brief separation. Although she would have preferred to discuss the events that led to his hasty exit, she had learned from past similar episodes: keep quiet, don't talk about it or Dominic will roar, and the problem will escalate. Feeling guilty that she was at fault for having driven him away, she also felt subservient. She craved his approval, his acceptance, his love. She prepared a nice dinner, and waited on him throughout the evening while he watched TV.

Early the next day they drove to Olive Canyon Resort because Dom had some work he wanted to do in the office there. His efforts on behalf of Olive Canyon were unpaid. He donated his labor for two reasons. First because Dominic knew he could accomplish what was necessary regarding the accounting and office management problems the club had been experiencing. Second because he wanted to give something back to the club that had provided him with many years of pleasure.

Doreen had moved the carton of tax receipts from her car's trunk to the Buick's, planning to sort them and get them in order for her IRS appointment while she was at camp. She dropped the heavy box on the floor of the mobile home next to the sofa where she could spread the papers out on the long coffee table to organize them. By lunchtime she had completed that task, and decided to spend a lazy afternoon swimming and socializing with all the other naked people.

In the quarter moon's feeble effort, the unlighted dirt road showed itself as a slightly paler ribbon than the surrounding black scrub. The Ford, headlights off, slowly ground along the familiar route, stopping, then turning left off the track to bounce through the low, scattered brush until it came to an open gate on the old, neglected, back-road exit that very few people knew about. A quarter of a mile farther, the driver shut off the engine, leaving the keys dangling. Easing the door open, the black-clad figure climbed down stealthily, and crept to the truck's tailgate, plucking out the two heavy cans of gasoline, the effort causing a suppressed grunt. Moving carefully, halting every few feet to listen and scan, all senses now keen as an owl's, the killer's target soon showed itself in the ancient olive grove. Onto the areas where it would best accomplish its mission, the noxious-smelling fluid was carefully dribbled. When the containers were empty, and after retreating a safe distance, the arsonist pulled paper matches from a pocket and lit one, using that to set fire to the match package, which was then thrown toward the narrow trail of gasoline leading to the intended target. Satisfied, the dark-robed murderer/arsonist grabbed a can in each hand and vanished into the darkness.

Doreen coughed, awoke smelling smoke, seeing fire advance, hearing the awful crackling sounds as combustion gobbled the mobile home. Flames climbed the bedroom drapes. Looking for a way to escape, dense black smoke rolled along under the low ceiling. Doreen hacked and choked, struggling for clear air to breathe. Terror engulfed her.

She yelled, "Dom!" and rattled his shoulder hard. "Fire! Wake up! We have to get out! Get down on the floor!" She pitched herself off the bed, landing on the thick padded carpet with a thud.

"Good God!" Dom rolled off the bed. Coughing, he crawled a few feet on his belly, his throat burning from inhaled smoke, with Doreen gasping beside him. Smoke, now thick everywhere, made visibility zero.

The door knob should be here. She reached up, feeling around for the hardware. A piece of flaming drapery bounced off her outstretched arm, and onto Dom's bare back.

He screamed, then rolled onto his back, smothering the fire. He coughed, and croaked out, "I'm okay. Let's get outta here!" as he turned back onto his hands and knees.

Flattening themselves like throw rugs to the floor, noses touching the carpet, their hands felt along the base of the wall for the door. By now the heat was intense. Sparks and whirling pieces of flaming material ignited patches of the bedding. Charred bits found bare backs to light on. The unrelenting din, the dense smoke that sanded throats and eyeballs, the fear of death—the taste of hell itself. They gasped and choked and coughed.

From her position on the floor Doreen found the door handle. "Got it! Come on!" The door opened. With the influx of outside air the fire roared, intensity increasing tenfold. Doreen squirmed out just as Dom shouted. She looked back. His hair was aflame. He was struggling to wrap it with a smoldering sheet. With one arm around his chest, Doreen dragged him out to safety. They smothered vestiges of fire in his smoking hair with the remains of the charred sheet.

Still choking and hacking, they sat on the cool dewy

morning ground, holding each other, naked except for the partially-blackened sheet wrapped around them, watching in numb shock as the fire blazed. The heat from it cooked them on the side facing the flames, cold damp air settled on the opposite side. Dawn's glow produced a hint of light from the eastern sky. About a hundred feet away, the gatekeeper-cabin's walls danced with the fire's flickering reflections.

"We're lucky to be alive," Dom rasped with great effort.

"Are you hurt much?" Doreen asked in a husky voice.

"No. I'm okay. I think we got the flames out quick enough." Dom hacked and hacked. His throat felt like it had glowing embers in it.

She shivered, speaking hoarsely. "I need something on besides this sheet, I'm getting cold. Let's rouse Katie and Howard—they'll have something we can wear. Better call the fire department, too."

Dom pounded several times on the door of the Brill's cabin. A sleepy nude Katie Brill answered, her hair in disarray. As she ushered Dom and Doreen in she shouted, "Howie, Howie!" While Howard called the fire department, Katie Brill made coffee and found robes for Doreen and Dom. From there they could see the roaring fire. Katie tisk-tisked at Doreen's burnt-off eyebrows, singed hair, and soot-smudged face, and led her to the shower.

When the fire department left, the mobile home was a distorted black evil-smelling horror. The Pierces, wearing borrowed ill-fitting clothing, drove to their home in Long Beach. They were exhausted from the physical and emotional trauma, and the lack of sleep.

Trying to rest, they found they couldn't. Too many questions. Was there a connection between the fire and Veronica's death? Had Doreen's snooping led the killer to think Doreen was getting too close to the answer? Who tried to kill them?

Poking among the steamy ashes, firemen found evidence of arson. Someone had dumped gasoline around the mobile. Someone was worried that the Pierces knew too much about Veronica's death.

Restless and tired, Doreen said over coffee, "I never should have asked so many questions. Now someone wants to kill us." She spread a bagel with strawberry jam. "I think the fire just proves beyond any doubt that Veronica was killed deliberately. I was right about that."

"Of course. It was no accident." Dominic finished the last bite of his bagel. "I warned you about this very possibility. Would you listen to me? No." Now he was bellowing. "You almost got me killed! And you too."

Doreen felt like cowering. Then the new Doreen emerged, sat with her head high, and said quietly, "Dominic. I did what I had to do. I'm sorry I pulled you into this—I was willing to take that risk by myself. I intend to continue doing what I feel is right."

Dom jumped up, his face flushed, yelling, "You'll get us both killed yet!" He turned and swept out of the room, muttering to himself.

Doreen felt wonderful! *I may be wrong, but I'll do what I feel is right. In one way I'm glad the fire happened. Now I know for certain Dom didn't kill Ronnie. What a relief to be sure about that!*

Somewhat recovered from the fire ordeal, the next day Doreen went to her Large Women's Fashions to check on the arrangements for the upcoming show. As she climbed out of her Honda in the parking lot, she remembered the box of receipts she had taken away to organize. They had been in the mobile home that burned to the ground with everything in it. Would the IRS agent accept her excuse that all her receipts were roasted in the fire? What to do? The deadline was only two days away! She tried and tried to telephone the IRS agent Ms. Gutterman to tell her about the fire. The line was always busy. Creases dented the skin between her brows, and her mouth pulled into a taut line. Without those receipts, dealing with Ms. Gutterman in two days would be frustrating and frightening.

Employees were careful to say nothing about Doreen's singed eyebrows, noticing that Doreen did not seem to be in her usual upbeat mood. She spent the day making calls, meeting with key employees, and helping arrange last-minute details for the show.

Chapter 21

The following Wednesday the Pierces drove to Olive
Canyon to spend the day. Doreen cringed as they drove
past the gutted, blackened mobile home—the strong,
acrid stench revived the night of terror. Doreen grabbed
Dom's arm, shuddering. He said, "It's over now."

Later, after a long, hot day at Olive Canyon Resort,
they went home to Long Beach, removing their clothes
as soon as they closed and locked the door, and turned
on several ceiling fans. Doreen made stuffed peppers
and angel-hair pasta with marinara sauce, and tossed a
salad of romaine lettuce, sweet onion slices, fresh
mushrooms, cucumber chunks, red bell pepper strips
and a dressing of balsamic vinegar and olive oil, their
favorite.

As soon as Dom stuffed a big bite of salad into his
mouth the phone rang. Since he was close enough to
pluck it off the wall-mounted base, he did so, handing it
to Doreen.

"Hello," she said.

"Detective Trappe here. How are you and Mr. Pierce?
I heard about the fire, and wanted to see how you and
your husband are doing."

"We're fine, thanks. I lost my eyebrows, but I'm okay.
What's new?" She held the receiver away from her ear so
that Dom, too, could hear. He leaned close to the receiver.

"I have some little news items I thought you two

might like to be aware of. I hope I haven't called at a bad time."

"No. I'm dying to hear your little news items—don't keep me in suspense."

"Until the fire I was pretty sure Jake Corrigan and Ruby Falstaff killed your cousin Veronica. Everything seemed to point that way. However, today I learned that when Mona Lott was only fourteen she set fire to the family home. No one was hurt, and it was put out quickly before it did much damage, but it makes me wonder. It seems the parents were too busy to pay attention to her, so she did it to get their attention. It worked, for a while anyway. They had her going to a therapist for a long time. She still gets depressed occasionally, and has to be treated."

"Wow! That *is* news."

"There's more. I suppose you knew that your friends the Lambs lost their son, their only child, about a year ago?"

"We had heard that. They stayed away from the resort for a long time."

"The young man was named Percy," the detective said. "He wrote a note, then hanged himself in their garage one night after they had gone to sleep. Apparently he was despondent over a lost love. No, not that, he said it was unrequited love. He just couldn't accept the fact that the lady was not returning his attention."

"Tell me, Detective, do you know if Percy Lamb was ever seen by a psychiatrist or a mental-health counselor?"

"I have his file here, just a minute." Soon he said, "It

looks like he went once to a counselor, but I don't have the report from that person."

"Can you give me his name?"

"Sure. Dr. Frank Castillo, in Lakewood."

"His death, Percy's I mean, must have been an awful blow to Angelo and Sarah. But I don't see how that has any connection to Veronica's death or the fire, do you?"

"No, not yet. I still don't have all the pieces to the puzzle, so I'll just file it away for now. That's how I work on a case."

Doreen said, "Here's another item for your files. One day before the fire we were at Olive Canyon. Dom was playing a volleyball game, so I went around chatting with people like I always do. I came across Ed and Mona Lott. Mona Lott asked me to go away from the others so we could talk—she had something to tell me in private. So I followed her up the path that leads to the chapel. When we got way away from the other people she turned around and started to tell me something, but she couldn't quite spit it out. She had me worried that she was planning to kill me by pushing me over the edge of the cliff and down into the canyon. That's a heck of a drop. Then she ran off, so I came back down alone. She's dying to tell me something, and I'm pretty sure she will, sooner or later."

"Will you tell me, Mrs. Pierce, what it is that's bothering her when you find out?"

"Sure. And why don't you call us Dominic and Doreen?"

"I will. I think we can help each other figure out who's behind the crimes."

"I hope the killer is caught soon—I'm worried about

someone setting fire to our home in Long Beach, or trying to kill us in some other way. Are you convinced now that Veronica was murdered?"

"Yes, although we have no proof, no evidence to link anyone to the crimes."

"I'm glad you, the police, are investigating. I felt everyone was content that my cousin died accidentally, and I couldn't accept that. I'm really anxious to see her killer behind bars, punished for her murder."

"Of course. That's it for tonight. Please let me or my partner Detective Jackson know of anything that might help."

"I will. Count on it. Thanks for calling."

In the morning Doreen was determined to find out more about Percy's session with Doctor Castillo in Lakewood. She found the doctor's address and telephone number in the directory. Now she needed a plan that would allow her a peek at the files. *Perhaps I'll impersonate a cop. No—too risky. A psychologist? Maybe. A social worker? Might work. How about a distraction? For that I'll need an accomplice—Ruby might help me. Ruby's been hounding me ever since the fire to let her help me with my snooping.*

She and Ruby concocted a strategy. Ruby would demonstrate to the receptionist a "new" product guaranteed to clean anything. If possible, Ruby would drag the person away to the rest room to show her how shiny the fixtures could become. If that wasn't possible, she'd spill the stuff and make a mess. Meanwhile, Doreen would raid the file cabinet for a glimpse at Percy's chart. To their amazement, the plan worked!

They discovered that Percy Lamb had suffered from

"paranoid jealousy" — the same as ordinary jealousy, but more profound and relentless. He projected his own wishes and desires onto his "love," thus convincing himself she was as infatuated with him as he was with her. Emotional incongruity — the outcome of his belief that his "love" cared for him, as evidenced by the attention she paid him — was another segment of his difficulty.

Doreen lay awake a long time after she crawled into bed that night, pondering something Felix Trappe had said. Something that had clicked in her mind, like it was pointing to the killer. What was it? She reconstructed each statement he had made, hoping for a repeat click. Suddenly she remembered stuffing the note from Sarah in the side pocket of her purse where it had remained. She dashed to the hallway table where she'd left her pocketbook, and felt for the square of paper. Positive she had a crucial piece of the puzzle, her hands quaked as she read:

I can't live with this pain anymore. You must know how much I love you. You must see it in my eyes. You're so nice to me. You talk to me. Every day I went to work hoping you would tell me I was special to you, but no. I love you too much not to have you for my own. I know you have a husband. You could divorce him.
Goodbye to you, my fair lady.

Chapter 22

She slid back under the covers. Dom, a sound sleeper, hadn't moved. Her mind focused on the words written on the scrap of paper. *Was he referring to a woman he worked with? Must be. Who else would be a possibility? Who was that woman? Could she have been Ronnie? Yes! It was when he said something about his "fair lady." "Unrequited love." Fair lady—Ronnie was very fair, light skin, light hair, blue eyes, pretty. A fair lady, to be sure. How would Percy have known her well enough to believe he was in love with her? Where did they cross paths? That's the missing piece in this puzzle.* Doreen's mind was like drops of water on a hot griddle when she realized she had the answer. She flopped around in the bed. *Of course! Percy would have seen her every day at work when he bought his lunch—from Corrigan's catering van! If that's the answer, then Angelo or Sarah or both of them killed Ronnie to avenge Percy's suicide. But how can I prove it?* Deciding that she'd share this revelation with either Detective Trappe or Detective Jackson first thing in the morning, she rehashed the details time and again to be sure every event meshed with the time of every other. Satisfied that she was right, she eventually dozed off.

Dom listened to her theory while he sat watching Doreen cook breakfast. He agreed it sounded plausible. She was so wound up she couldn't eat, so instead, she told the detectives triumphantly. Detective Trappe congratulated her on her discovery, and told her he'd get back to her later that day.

Doreen got ready, and drove again to visit Sarah at the hospital. She poked her head into Sarah's room, hoping Angelo wasn't there. The room smelled sterile, as if it did not contain a human being. Sarah was alone, with oxygen and gastric tubes and IVs and beeping monitors to keep her company. Stepping up next to the bed, Doreen took Sarah's warm plump hand and held it, realizing how much weight her friend had lost. There was no movement, so she spoke quietly to her. No response.

A male nurse wearing a pin that read "George Karistopolis, R.N." came in. He said, "She's comatose. She may or may not hear you—she's completely unresponsive."

"Can you tell me what's wrong with her? What the tests showed?"

"Are you family?" He was studying the monitor screens.

"Yes," Doreen lied, justifying the lie by telling herself she wouldn't tell anyone else what she was about to hear in this hospital room.

"Mrs. Lamb has an inoperable brain tumor. The prognosis is poor."

"Poor dear." Doreen turned and hurried out. She felt devastated. *Another death for Angelo to face. First his only son, soon his wife. If he is the person who killed Ronnie, I despise him for that. But I feel sorry for him too.*

The crowded sitting room of the swing-party house crackled with tension. The lighting was much brighter than on party nights. Everyone who had been present when Veronica died was here tonight—at Detective

Jackson's request—and in addition, there were uniformed police stationed at the doors, in the front, back, and side yards, and several more inside the house.

Police Detective Tawnia Jackson, an amazon of a woman with taut dark skin and pretty black eyes, loathed people like these—swingers. With AIDS around, they were just plain fools, in her opinion. But her job required her to be here. Detective Felix Trappe was there, too.

Some of the swingers sipped on soft drinks or coffee, some talked in subdued tones, a few showed their annoyance at this command performance by scowling in silence. Doreen and Dom waited nervously for the drama to start. After all, Doreen had convinced Detective Jackson to set up this gathering, with no assurance that it would net a confession. The detective studied her papers for a few minutes after the last couple arrived, checking off each name on her list as she located the matching person.

"Good. You're all here, so we can begin." Tawnia Jackson's black eyes sparkled with excitement. This wrap-up would boost her career if it resulted in putting the murderer behind bars. She felt like keeping her fingers crossed, but thought better of it. Her tall, sturdy frame unfolded as she stood up, smiling broadly, beautiful white teeth contrasted by her crimson lipstick and attractive sepia complexion.

"The first thing I want to say to all of you is this: thanks for showing up tonight. I'm sure you're as eager as I am to find Mrs. Corrigan's killer."

Comments and murmurs came from the assembled group, such as, "Killer? I thought it was an accident."

"Come with me, Mrs. Falstaff." The detective led Ruby to the Group Room where a card table and two folding chairs waited, and a tape recorder. The floor had been cleared of the mattresses that had covered it last time Dory saw the room. Two floor lamps brightened the area. As they sat on opposite sides of the table, Detective Jackson switched the tape recorder on and asked, "Who were you with around 10 p.m. on the night Veronica Corrigan died?"

"I spent some time with Jake first, and then later with Dick Weiner, probably around ten."

"Thank you." Detective Tawnia Jackson wrote on the paper in front of her. Keeping a noncommittal expression on her face she said, "Please send Mr. Avery Trent in."

Returning to the sitting room Ruby felt lightheaded with relief that her grilling was over, and it had been so brief. She whispered to Avery that he was next. Avery Trent, a very average forty-ish man with a long jaw and an angular nose, was nervous being this close to police and a murder scene. The evening before the party he'd been alone at a bar psyching himself up to approach Ruby. To his amazement she moved over and sat next to him, smiled, and started a conversation. *It's a miracle,* he'd thought, *I'm so plain-looking, and she's anything but plain—she's gorgeous.* After a while she asked him if he'd like to attend a swing party with her, explaining that she would not be admitted solo, and she wanted to go to it as some of her old friends would be there. When he heard this he knew all his prayers had been answered, and wondered if something hallucinogenic had been dropped into his whiskey. His first swing party on the following night delivered him to Camelot or Heaven or

Nirvana, for a while anyway, until the body was discovered.

Ruby nudged him out of his musings whispering, "She's waiting for you."

He finished off his soda in one gulp, stood up, and tucked his shirt in tighter before going into the room with the detective. When he was seated, Detective Jackson repeated the question she had asked of Ruby. He replied, and she asked him to send in the next person on her list.

One by one the suspects answered the question: Who were you with around 10 p.m. on the night Veronica Corrigan was killed? By questioning them separately, and cross-checking names and times—provided that these replies were truthful—the persons who had had the opportunity to commit the murder would be pinpointed. Of course, this questioning didn't prove a thing, but it served an important function, that of giving the killer the feeling that justice was closing in, or so Detectives Trappe and Jackson hoped. A taped confession by the perp would be cause for celebration.

Doreen observed the others, watching for telltale body language, extreme nervousness, anything to pinpoint a murderer. Everyone seemed uneasy, probably wanting to get this thing over, Doreen decided, and not understanding why they had been asked to this location instead of police headquarters.

Detective Jackson, having completed the first segment of the plan, strode back to the waiting people—some merely curious, some agitated—and said, "Now, let's all go out to the pool." A murmur of "no" came from several women, horrified by the memory of seeing Veronica's body the previous time when they'd crowded out to see what all the commotion was about. Although Doreen helped plan this setup, had steeled herself in advance for it, she nevertheless became queasy about viewing the scene again.

Dom led the way, everyone straggling along behind him to flock just outside the sliding doors. It was very dark, just as it had been the night Veronica died. The little shaded lights set back two feet from the pool gave only the faintest illumination, and that only at ground level. As everyone's eyes adjusted, they could discern dark blobs they recognized as chairs, tables, and shrubs. The pool's surface was an ebony mirror of the night sky. Beside the pool lay a dark lump of towel with a prosthetic foot sticking out.

Upon recognizing the prosthesis Doreen sobbed, and several people, including Angelo, gasped.

Chapter 23

Pent-up guilt exploded in great sobs as Angelo shouted, "No. No. It can't be! She's dead!"

Several officers rushed toward him. Angelo threw his left arm around Doreen's neck. She screamed, "Help!" He tightened his arm on her neck, pulled her close to shield himself. His right hand grasped a wicked knife, poised against the side of her bare throat. She heard several people suck in their breath in shock.

Yelling, "Don't come near me!" he held the glinting steel against Doreen's skin. Overwhelming terror made her cooperate—he had already tried to kill her by fire. She felt her insides turn to jelly, and her legs threatened to let her sag downward. Summoning her utmost strength she held herself motionless, feeling the sharp blade's sting on her neck where it had nicked her soft skin. She felt a trickle of warm blood. Angelo's hold disabled her attempted scream.

In a low authoritative voice Detective Trappe said, "Come on now. Give me that knife and let her go. You're outnumbered here. You can't get away."

"I'll kill her. Get away, all of you!"

No one moved. The tableau was frozen in place.

Angelo backed away a few steps, dragging Doreen with him like a big, stuffed teddy bear. She felt the sharp steel bite. Pain seared her flesh. Terror seared her mind. In desperation, she tried to lunge down and to her right,

132

away from the weapon. Angelo retaliated by securing her head more tightly in the vise of his muscular shoulder and forearm.

Doreen could see only sky. Breathing was almost impossible. She told herself to suck air in slowly and carefully to prevent motion that would deepen the knife's gory work. She smelled his garlic and wine-laden breath, and his sweat. Also her own blood. Her arms hung limp.

From behind, a small scratching sound. A siren screamed. Angelo swung his head around, loosening the vice ever so slightly. Doreen burst against his arms with both hands, ducking downward.

From near her head came the explosion of a quick gunshot, then another. Angelo jolted with each blast. She felt herself falling forward, wondered if she'd been hit. She felt no pain now. *Am I dead?* Angelo blanketed her, not moving. Reaching back, her fingers ran into stickiness on Angelo's face. She knew. She shivered. Not knowing where the noise came from, she heard a wailing scream erupt from deep down inside her.

Suddenly Angelo's weight was gone, and helping hands pulled her up from both sides. Like a camera shutter closing, blackness swept across her vision. As she fainted, two officers caught her and laid her gently on the ground.

Someone was taking her pulse when she heard Jake Corrigan cry out, "He killed my Veronica. It wasn't an accident. He killed her!" He wept with great heaving sobs. "I wish I'd shot him."

Doreen whispered, "Me too." She was crying when she got back on her feet, and then Ruby was holding her, as Doreen had held Ruby when Elliott died. Dominic stood scowling on the other side of her, hands in his pockets. Doreen pulled herself together and said, "You know, he didn't confess. I hope he isn't dead—he needs to confess."

Ruby said, "You're right. He didn't ever say he killed Veronica."

In the back of the ambulance with two police officers, a paramedic, and Angelo, Doreen sat, weak and pale, with a bandaged neck. Angelo was alive, but unconscious, his head and shoulder wrapped in thick gauze through which blood still seeped. He was strapped down to the gurney, and had IV fluids running into the back of his right hand.

At the emergency room, Angelo was rushed away. Doreen's neck scratch was superficial, so after it was cleaned and dressed, she was released. She left with Dominic and Ruby who had followed the ambulance in Dominic's car.

CHAPTER 24

The Long Beach house was a welcome sight. Soon after they finished eating a light supper, the phone rang. It was Mona Lott, wanting to talk with Doreen. She asked how Doreen was doing. Doreen told her the neck wound was just a bad scratch, healing well.

"I just couldn't face you and tell you," Mona said, "but I really do want to, so I thought it might be easier on the phone. So hear goes. I hope you won't think I'm crazy or anything, but after Veronica won the election, I was terribly upset. More than anyone knew. I had been so sure I'd win. But I didn't. Do you remember she had a flat tire, and Jake had to put the spare tire on so they could go home? *I* did it! I let the air out of her tire."

"Mona, you can't imagine what a relief it is to hear that."

"Relief? I'm glad you're taking it so well. I've been feeling like a criminal since then. What did you think I was about to confess?"

"I hate to say this, but I thought for a while you might have killed Veronica."

"Me? Good God! I could never kill anybody or anything. Except sometimes maybe myself."

For a few more minutes, Mona asked Doreen questions about the time bomb, Veronica's murder, the fire, Angelo, then rang off.

Doreen called the medical center in Los Angeles to

inquire about Sarah. She learned that Sarah had expired that day. Angelo had died without regaining consciousness.

As she put down the phone her thoughts jumped back to the day she kept her appointment with the IRS. She had prepared for her scheduled meeting with the IRS agent by assembling as many papers as she could find for that year in question, 2001. The fire had destroyed all her business receipts, but she had found some penciled notes she'd made. She did not ask Dominic to accompany her since he had other pressing matters of his own to attend to that afternoon, and more importantly, she wanted to stand on her own two feet to prove to herself she could. Having recently recognized how often she had gladly placed herself in her husband's shadow, she was determined now to grasp at opportunities to experience her own strength.

Upon entering the cubicle at IRS, she was unnerved to find that her correspondent Ms. Gutterman had been replaced by a man. A cold gray steel desk separated her from a large heavyset person whose extra-short black hair grew straight out from his head like bristles. On the desk the black plastic plaque read Hornbull Stern. Fidgeting, she waited while he slid his saggy gray eyes over the few pages she handed him. His thick black eyebrows met in the middle of his face and his chair squealed when he moved. She chewed on her fingernail stubs, just barely resisting the urge to down a chocolate bar.

"Mrs. Pierce, this material looks fine, but according to my copy of the letter, this is the wrong year. We're interested in your 2002 tax return. Did you bring it?" He waved the papers at her.

"2002! Really?" She squirmed, blushing and feeling like a worm under a microscope. "Good heavens. I must have read your letter wrong. All along I've been thinking you wanted to see 2001. I had all the receipts at home in a box to put them in order, but the fire destroyed them—the 2001 ones. I've almost got an ulcer worrying about it."

Grim faced he said, "I'll give you until Tuesday to get the 2002 return and receipts to me. I hope we won't need to see 2001."

"I have all those receipts at my place of business. I'll bring them in to you tomorrow afternoon." She departed on still-trembling legs but with a sigh of relief. Getting into her car, she realized she was desperate for a cup of coffee to moisten her dry mouth, so she pulled in to the first coffee shop in sight. After two mugs and some time to calm herself, she felt ready to tackle the final preparations for tomorrow's fashion show.

Returning to Large Women's Fashions, she entered by the rear door. The first person to cross her path made her eyes light up.

"Roberto. You're back! Just in time to make sure the show goes well." Dory had a hard time keeping herself from hugging her errant employee. "How was Hawaii?"

"Ah, I, ah, felt so guilty leaving everything for you to handle, when I had promised you I would do it." He paused, seeming genuinely contrite. Then his charming grin erased her apprehension about the show. "Hawaii was the same as ever, fantastic. Even so, I'm glad to be back. The show must go on!"

"I'm glad too. Tomorrow's almost here, and we still have a lot to do."

"Don't fret. It will be just fabulous, flawless as always." Roberto threw both arms toward Doreen and danced a few tango steps. "You'll see."

And it was.

Chapter 25

Two evenings later Doreen had settled down in her favorite reading chair with John Steinbeck's *Travels with Charley*.

Dom unlocked the door and walked in saying, "I'm home."

"We need to talk," Doreen said in a stern tone, without smiling. She put a marker in the book she'd been reading and set the book down, rolling her tucked-up feet down to the floor so she could sit up straight.

"OK, shoot." He folded his lanky frame onto an easy chair opposite hers.

"I've given a lot of thought to our relationship lately, Dom. I think we'd both be better off living apart permanently." Dom seemed shocked. She brushed her hand across her forehead saying, "You don't need to answer right now—give it some thought. The way I see it, we can continue to be friends if we're not living together. I'd like to separate while we can still get along. I care for you too much to let us come to hating each other. There's no reason to become enemies, which is what will happen if we stay together much longer."

After a long pause he said, "I'm surprised to hear this. But I'll think about it." He knew her well enough to understand by her expression and tone that she had made a decision and would not budge.

A month later Dominic moved out for good. He and Doreen remained amiable. One day Dom phoned Doreen to say, "Guess what! I'm keeping four women happy in bed these days. And I never thought I was a ladies' man."

Doreen thought, *Is he telling me this to hurt me?* However, she muttered aloud in reply, "Good for you, Dom." *He's still a misogynist—he won't change.*

After about four months of living apart, Doreen filed for divorce. Dominic did not contest it. Custody of their beloved sailboat *Windcatcher* was to be every other week as if it were their child, other arrangements by agreement. They divided all other possessions to their mutual satisfaction.

Ruby and Doreen continued to be close friends.

"Isn't this a glorious day to be out here on the ocean?" Doreen asked while opening the Styrofoam cooler. Pulling several cans of V8 juice out, she passed one to Roger, the man next to her, and two to Ruby. Roger Katz, Doreen's recent acquaintance, was manning the tiller.

"It's just perfect," Ruby said smiling, and handing a can of V8 juice to Jake Corrigan, sitting next to her in the cockpit of the sloop.

Looking at Doreen, Roger said, "Couldn't be better."

The sun shone. The breezes filling *Windcatcher's* sails kept the boat slicing through the sparkly sea at about five knots, heeling at a comfortable angle. The saltwater smell invigorated the sailors. Spirits soared as the crew kidded each other, told jokes and relaxed.

It had been two years since Elliott Falstaff's death, and almost as long since Doreen's cousin Veronica Corrigan had been murdered. The pain of loss was a little duller now. Wonderful days like these helped heal the emotional wounds, and Doreen, Ruby, and Jake found solace in new loves. Ruby Falstaff and Jake Corrigan delighted in one another's companionship, having many common interests including sunbathing and swinging. Roger was a widower who had enjoyed the nudist lifestyle with his wife in Maryland.

Months ago at one of the dances at Olive Canyon, Doreen and Roger rocked and rolled to "Mack the Knife." Then the live four-piece band played a swing tune, "In the Mood," and they danced to that. When they sat at a table to catch their breath and cool off, a spark ignited between them.

Seeing Doreen at the dance, Roger had found her physically attractive—trim figure, pretty face, long dark hair. Doreen had changed: since divorcing Dominic, no longer did she gobble chocolate, no longer did she chew her fingernails, no more nightmares, no more poor self-image. She realized her emotional problems had been due to the relationship with Dominic. When Roger became better acquainted with Doreen, he admired her personality too, because she was spunky, happy, and confident.

After a few happy hours of sailing, they turned the sailboat toward home. Tying the boat into its slip at the marina, the four sailors picked up their clothes and coolers and set them on the dock. Doreen hosed the boat with fresh water from a nearby tap after locking the hatch, while Ruby covered the lowered sails. They picked up their things to lug them to the car. As they bounced along the floating wooden walkways, Doreen and Ruby sang, "Row, row, row your boat gently down the stream." The four of them belted out, "Merrily, merrily, merrily, merrily, life is but a dream."

Printed in the United States
40396LVS00002B/24

9 781413 724271